THE
LONG
MIDNIGHT

THE

LONG

MIDNIGHT

ALAN WHITE

HARCOURT BRACE JOVANOVICH, INC.
NEW YORK

Printed in the United States of America

Library of Congress Cataloging in Publication Data

White, Alan.
    The long midnight.

    I. Title.
PZ4.W5827Lq3   [PR6073.H49]   823'.9'14
ISBN 0-15-153075-0   73-13952

First American edition 1974
B C D E

for

FRANK, who flew a glider,

FRANK, who tapped a key,

FRANK, who jumped,

and all the others.

He was still there, standing on a rock at the edge of the fjord. The moon marked out the steel helmet which fitted low over his ears, and glowed from the buckles of his leather strapped equipment, the signet ring on the middle finger of his right hand, and the magazine of the machine-gun he carried loosely under one arm ready to lift and fire. He was wearing a dark-green uniform and knee-length boots that would be padded inside for warmth. He'd need those boots before dawn broke. I had never been so cold.

Though it was impossible, as I kept telling myself, it felt as if water from the fjord had seeped inside my pod, the one-man submarine built of packing-case plywood and sewn together with string. You caulk them with tarred canvas melted with a blowlamp and moulded to fit. You can make them any shape you like.

I'd never made one for sub-surface work before but with a simple air escape valve to send me quickly down and an air bottle to bring me back up again, I had been confident I could get into the Norwegian fjords. And I'd been right: this was the Sognefjord and I'd brought myself all the way along it! That'll be one in the eye for Commander Disbelieving Carter of the Royal Navy, I thought.

The air bottle I carried was made of neoprene rubber and had been invented in 1942 by a boffin in Manchester University. My escape valve was also made of rubber. A wooden shell without nails, a rubber bottle and valves, Innsbrucker boots with specially glued and sewn soles, and me lying full-length inside the pod: nothing metal to give a blip on the radar we knew the Germans now possessed.

7

The snag was that I couldn't take a gun or a knife, or even a piano-wire garrote with me. With luck I'd find them, if ever I got out of the fjord, beneath the rock where that blasted German was standing. He had a black Labrador beside him, and they're the worst kind of dog. They're not vicious, they'll never attack you, but they have a nose as keen as a bloodhound and a lolloping run that carries then barking to wherever you're hiding.

My arms stretched out of the holes in the sides of the pod, clad in rubber sleeves and mitts sealed to the wooden frame. I located the picture cord that connected me to Sergeant Milner's pod. One pull meant stay down, two meant get the hell farther down, three meant come up. I pulled once, then started forward again. Damn, my arms were exhausted; I couldn't use the foot pedal that operated the vanes in the tail of the pod because the shaft seemed to have jammed and I couldn't risk forcing it free in case I broke the rubber seal.

We were two miles from our launching point off the coast of Norway above Bergen. It was February 1943; and at twenty-six I must have been one of the youngest lieutenant-colonels in the British Army. I'd been promoted from Lieutenant, Acting Captain, and I hadn't quite believed them when they told me why.

The German was looking out over the water, but I was sure he couldn't see me. The pod was covered with bark that extended even over the observation bubble on the top of each side, giving me a row of slits through which I could see clearly when the small waves didn't splash. On the surface, even from close up, the pod would look like a half-submerged log floating in the fjord. The boffins had even designed a vane on the air release valve that chopped up the bubbles and spread them less conspicuously over a larger area. The pod was weighted all along its spine with a length of concrete. In our early tests on Ellesmere some clown had reinforced the concrete with half an inch of iron

8

bar, and the pod had winked at the radar screens from two miles away.

The German didn't seem in any hurry to move. The dog squatted beside him, licking its front paw. What the hell was a Labrador doing in Norway, anyway?

I drove the pod slowly along the surface. The German was about a hundred yards away; I was well within range of that automatic. Once or twice Sergeant Milner's pod dragged on the line, but he quickly adjusted his pace to keep a loop in front of him, the way we'd practised. I didn't want him dragging my pod down, making ripples where no ripples ought to be. I dared not go too far along the fjord; I'd passed Vik some time ago and the bank ahead swung out to the Balestrand ferry. My major sight bearing was to line up the tip of the Jostedalsbreen, 6,000 feet high to the left and ahead, with the tip of land where it curved out from the right; once I lost that sight line I'd have no easy way to locate the exact arrival point on the bank and a cache of food and weapons.

The pod wasn't fitted with a zipper; it'd take many helpless moments to get out of it. I stopped paddling, took my right arm back into the pod and for the hundredth time reached down to grasp the suitcase latch with which the two halves were held together. One good pull and the latch would spring inwards, the rubber seals would burst apart, and I could push the top of the pod backwards over my head then scramble out of the bottom half. When we'd rehearsed this move on Ellesmere they'd fired Bren guns over our heads; it was terrifying to realise how many bullets they could put around us during that one simple move.

I'd have felt better if that damned moon hadn't been glaring down on us, if the German hadn't been standing on the rock with a Labrador by his side, if I were still on Ellesmere, and if Sergeant Milner hadn't beaten me out of the pod by at least half a magazine every time ... I hadn't notified Milner that I'd stopped, and he'd carried on ahead

9

of me. His line jerked me forward, yanking my chin against the strap of the head cradle. I put my arm back into the the sleeve, located the taut line, and pulled it to tell him to stop. The line came slack in my hand as I used its tautness to ease forward. Then I started paddling again and gave him the signal to follow.

His was the hardest job, number two on the line, submerged for part of the way with no idea of where he was or what was happening, using his air bottle all the time and wondering just how long it would last, how much air was left in there to breathe. Most of the way along the Sognefjord we'd travelled on the surface, side by side, breathing through ventilator tubes with our bottles switched off. Three times he'd submerged when German-driven power boats had come too close for comfort. Once I'd submerged with him when one boat, inexplicably, had stopped close by and it had seemed as if one of the ratings was going to throw a grapple anchor across my pod. Apart from that incident, our journey had been cold but uneventful. I didn't mind that; I didn't crave excitement, only to arrive in one piece.

I manoeuvred the pod closer to the shore. Ideally, we needed a rocky shelf on which to land. A man could lift his own pod if he could get a good grip and we'd become quite skilled at rolling across flat rocks out of the water. Under the lee of the rock I lost sight of the German and hoped I would be out of range of his dog's nose. I trundled slowly along the shore line, looking for a place to land. There were fifty yards of shingle but that was useless, ten yards of towering rock which doubtlessly ran sheer down through the water. Then I came on the sort of place I was looking for, low rocks at the water line, rock beneath the surface. The pod bumped gently as I eased it forward across a flat rock table with my arms stretched out. A jagged rock lay ahead, but to its side was a long low channel, with rocks I could use to drag myself along. Quick

10

look in all directions. No-one in sight. Dammit, we ought
to have worked out a way to hear inside the pod, maybe
with an acoustic funnel we could have fitted into our ears
like a gramophone horn in reverse. Look again through the
vision slits; moon's bright and that means some Charlie
could be watching through a rifle sight from fifty yards
away, tucked in snug behind a rock, or lying on a pine-
needle carpet at the base of those trees directly ahead.
What would he think of a tree trunk that brought itself
ashore? Even if my sleeves were covered with artificial
moss? If ever I do this again, I thought, I'll make the pod
in four sections joined together like the scales of a cocoon,
so the pod can bend along its length.

I was stuck between two rocks. I reached as far ahead as
I could, grasped the rocks and pulled. No, the back of the
pod was stuck. Lie absolutely still and don't panic. Push
backwards to try to free the pod. No, it won't go backwards
either. Right, turn your arms round, don't panic, and try
to twist yourself free. Left hand down, pushing, right hand
up, pulling. Still the pod wouldn't move. Sweat poured
along my back. Damn. The inside of my rubber gloves was
clammy, and my hands slipped. Damn! I withdrew one
hand. The glove tried to turn itself inside out, sticking to
my hand, but I managed to pull it off. Close the air bottle;
close the valve. Release the other hand. I felt for and found
the neoprene suitcase latch. We'd practised all kinds of
release, under water, on the water, half in the water.
Though you don't realise it your body becomes compara-
tively warm inside the pod and the first rush of cold air
can make you gasp. You feel cold, but in reality you're a
lot warmer than the cold outside. I sprang the latch,
heard the rubber seals part and the phrrrt of air being
released, and then felt the chattering cold as air gushed
in around my middle. I pushed the top of the pod backwards and upwards and jerked myself forwards, sliding
along the flat stone, forwards and out.

11

Quick look around. Nothing. No sign of anyone. No crack of bullets. No shouts from the trees, no whispers from the rocks. I tried crouching; my legs held me though they'd had no real exercise since the vanes packed up ten miles back. I dragged the pod across the stones, tipped the ends to pour out the water, then sealed it again with the outside suitcase latch. I crawled to the lip of the rock to where I could look along the shore line in the direction of the German. No sign of him. The shore line was strewn with rocks. Mostly the rock went sheer down into the fjord, but occasionally a fall of rubble had built a promontory which had settled down, fifteen or twenty feet into the water. Still no sign of anyone. Watch and wait, watch and wait.

So far, if anyone is watching me, they only know one man is here. They don't know that another man in another pod lurks out there. I was wearing an ordinary khaki tweed uniform. We'd tried all manner of oilskins, but they had all overheated inside the pod; we'd tried long combinations, but they had proved too cold. My uniform was wet with sweat, even though I'd had the minimum of liquid for the few days before departure and had exercised strenuously to get the water content of my body as low as possible.

The air was cold and crisp; there was snow on the hills immediately above the tree line, which in some places reached down to the water's edge. Dark shadows in the pines; a quiet, intensely quiet night. It must have been about four o'clock. A flight of mallard came down the far hillside and swooped silent across the water. Mallard, or were they teal? Perhaps that was what the German had been waiting for; perhaps he was a bird fancier.

So far as we had known back in England, the shores of the Sognefjord were not patrolled along this south side. A small German garrison was stationed at Vik, another at Leikanger across the fjord with a section, three men only, in Fresvik. This man could be from Vik, which didn't seem likely, or from Fresvik, though that was at least twelve miles away. What the devil was he doing there, standing on the very rock beneath which my supplies had been hidden? The rock was unmistakable from the fjord—that's why we had picked it. Flat in the centre, with two pinnacles like devil's ears, one at each end. It looked like the flat top of a head. I hadn't been wrong. Dammit, I'd seen a photograph of it, and I couldn't mistake it.

One last look around; nothing in sight. Nothing. I grasped the cord from my pod and gave the signal on it. Then I started to haul him in, slowly. Now he'd have his bottle open to blow air into the pod to give him buoyancy. I stopped pulling to give him time to rise to the surface, and though I was expecting him, I felt a small shock when he suddenly rose through the water. Part of the bark had stripped off the celluloid window on the near side. The moonlight would shine on that. He was about twenty feet out. I drew him slowly in, looking constantly about me, along the rocks, back into the tree line. Night time searching is a matter of instinct more than vision. You don't have a hope in hell of seeing a man, even in bright moonlight, if he stays still in a patch of shadow. The blacks are black as pitch and the whites are too bright to help you. Instinct, however, will usually give you the feel of a piece of ground. You know if a human being is watching you, if unseen eyes are focused on you. Your skin knows and prickles; your hair knows and sits wrong on your scalp; your fingers itch. I had no reaction to the ground about me. That's dangerous. My nerve ends could have been dulled after such a long time in the boat. We'd been in those pods for forty-eight hours. We'd slept in them, eaten in them, and performed our natural functions in bags strapped front and back in them.

When Sergeant Milner's pod broached the rock there was a slight bump and another segment of bark tore away.

13

I could see where my pod had caught and steered him clear. He fastened the suitcase latch of his pod without speaking and we took off our boots, gaiters, trousers and underpants. I rolled my shirt up round my waist, then slithered forward over the rock into the water. Sergeant Milner stood beside me, the relief on his face obvious as we tore off the bags and dropped them into the water before washing ourselves. He was a fastidious man and to live in contact with his own excreta must have appalled him.

We pushed the pods back into the water and watched them sink under the weight of the concrete stiffeners. I brought the cord up under an overhanging rock face and secured it there. It was heavily oiled and waxed; it would hold for a few days. We were wading out of the water, shirts held round our waists, and bottom parts of our bodies exposed, when the German stepped out from behind a rock. The Labrador was at his side, growling.

"You will put up your hands," the German said in English. As I did so my shirt dropped to curtain my exposed parts. Too late I told myself I ought to have continued farther down the fjord round the point. But I'd been scared of losing the line between the mountain and the tip. Once past that line, I'd thought we'd never find the exact rock under which my supplies, food and weapons were hidden. And I badly had needed the comfort of a pistol in my hands.

All this way, for nothing. How long had we been in those damned pods, for nothing? We could have jumped in by parachute, or they could have landed us in a light plane. But no, the Brigadier had said in his office in Maida Vale, cups of Army tea every hour on the hour in private Minton, no, you must get in with no chance whatsoever of detection by either the Germans or the Norwegians themselves. That was why we'd practised day after day on Ellesmere, gone through a physical hardening course,

14

brought our pods through the defences that spanned the mouth of the Sognefjord, the minefields, the radar scanners, and all the long way up the fjord itself for what I estimated to be forty hours, since they don't make rubber watches. Only three men of unimpeachable reputation knew a job was on, and not even they knew the details. They'd been instructed by clandestine radio to put arms and supplies under that rock on which the German had stood. Had they been clumsy? Had they led the German, on a suspicion, right to our arrival point?

Now I knew why they'd promoted me to Lieutenant-Colonel. To boost the pension they'd pay to that wife of mine.

I married Betty in 1941, shortly after I got home from Denmark in an escaped fishing boat. I was supposed to be in the bag with thousands of others left behind to fight the rearguard action at Dunkirk; but I've never been much good at accepting my fate without making a fight of it. I stayed with the Royal Artillery as long as we had a unit, and then took off on my own. Most of the escapees were heading for Spain and Portugal. I knew the Germans had a net around the southern side of the carnage on the beach, so I went north, through Belgium, up into Germany by Neumünster, Kiel and Schleswig, and crossed the border at Flensburg. I'd worked in Swedish and Danish tanneries before the war; I'm six feet one inch and have blond hair; I had no problems so long as I stayed in the crowds. I finally got onto a boat at Agger, up in the north of Denmark near Nykøbing, and we landed at Great Yarmouth.

Betty was waiting for me in Gillingham, and we were married in a tiny church overlooking the Medway. If I'd known what was good for me, I'd have jumped in the river. There's a poem in Spanish called "The Unfaithful Wife". One of the lines is, 'she told me she was a virgin when I took her by the river'. Lorca had the man in the poem give her a basket of silks and ribbons to show he knew she was a tart; I didn't hear what a tart Betty was until we'd been married six months and I was training recruits back in the depot at Maidstone. I took Betty to the Regimental Dance one Saturday evening. She was doing the foxtrot with my Company Commander and I was standing at the bar getting myself some Dutch courage, when an officer who'd been away on a long course and

16

didn't know me said to his drinking pal, "Oh, she's back in circulation, is she? The Mess will be pleased."

"Sergeants' or Officers'?"

"It never used to matter to Bedworthy Betty in the old days. She'd even take 'em out of the N.A.A.F.I."

Bedworthy Betty. My wife.

I broke the man's jaw. Poor bastard; it wasn't his fault he'd ridden the regimental bicycle.

The C.O. was very decent about it. They were asking for volunteers for Special Services and he let me go. If I could have found Betty again, after I kicked her out that night, I would have divorced her, though I would have had to quote the entire regiment as co-respondents. The Pay Office would hear from her soon enough. As soon as I was posted missing, believed killed in action.

Sergeant Milner and I walked slowly forward, by instinct. The nearer you get the better your chance of taking a gun away, but the German was wise to that one. "That is sufficiently near," he said. The dog was still growling.

"May we get dressed?" I asked.

The German nodded. There was no need for him to warn us. At that distance we couldn't rush him, or even use a pistol if we'd had one. All I had was a wooden butcher's skewer stuck down the inside of a gaiter and a piece of thin oiled string with wooden toggles at each end, wound round my wrist. Sergeant Milner had a bamboo bow in three sections in the seam of his trousers, along with some arrows, but it would take him a while to get them out and fit them together. We dressed silently. There was nothing to say. I had a certain amount of hope. After all, he'd let us dress, hadn't he, which implied he was taking us somewhere before disposing of us. Obviously he wasn't an official greeting party. The Germans would never have left it to one man if they had known we were coming; at least a whole platoon would have been waiting for us. So who the hell was he, here on his own, with his dog?

"Thank you for letting us get dressed," I said suddenly in German. "We were very cold." He answered in German, in an accent with the soft sound of Bavaria.

"You have been in the water a long time," he said. "You must be very cold." He beckoned with the gun and we preceded him along the path, back towards Vik. When we had gone about two miles, he turned left, away from the fjord, and we began to climb through the timber line. The

18

snow was thick and powdery, the footprints of birds and animals everywhere. Snow hung in the branches of the pines, and occasionally crashed through the lower leaves with a faint rumbling sound. Once we were caught under such a snowfall; when I looked back, he had stopped and was waiting for us to clear ourselves of the light powdery drift. His gun was held ready.

Between Vik and Fresvik, the ground rises rapidly to a glacier about four miles in width. When we had climbed about a thousand feet, he beckoned us to go right, maintaining the same level. Behind us towered the glacier of the Jostedalsbreen beyond the Sognefjord; a wind blowing across its top lifted the snow as if it were cotton wool. My clothes had dried with the exertion of the climb and though I was cold walking kept my blood flowing and I felt no discomfort. The muscles at the back of my leg were pulling, but that would soon end the way a stitch goes away if you keep on running. I'd feel it in the morning if I lived that long.

While we walked, the moon slipped down behind the hills and the light faded. I looked back several times but he was keeping the right distance from us, close enough to watch every move we made, far enough back to make a run impossible. I'd worked the string garotte down into my right hand, with the toggles up my sleeve. As I walked I practised dropping it into my hand, ready for action. I saw Sergeant Milner fumbling with the cloth straps that held his bow down his leg, but it was too long to extract. Dawn broke suddenly on us while we were on a long traverse, shooting blood red lights into the sky, lining the cotton wool clouds. At each step the light changed, a moving panorama of colours that melted subtly into each other, reds and yellows, fiery white on the edges, blue in the sky occasionally revealed beyond. It was a spectacular welcome to a new day; I was not confident I would see the night fall again except once, and for all time.

Rounding a bend we came upon a small hut, probably used by a farmer during the summer when he brought his cattle up to the saeter. Now the cattle would all be down in the valley in the stabburs, or on the German Officers' Mess tables. The hut was made of wood with a high pitched roof, also of wood. Where the wind had blown off the snow, we could see that the eaves were notched and holed in a pattern that resembled cake icing. The door was set back in a small porch, also roofed in this decorative pattern, and the door itself was made of thick planks no doubt to withstand the kicks of animals.

The door was not locked. The German motioned for us to open it but when we started inside he stopped us. "Come back out here," he said, "and lie down." We did as we were told while he went in. We heard the creak of a window opening. "You can come in," he said.

As we walked in, he switched his aim from outside to inside. He was well trained and cautious. I lit the fire, and Sergeant Milner went into the cupboard and brought out goat cheese, herring, flat bread, and coffee which he brewed in a kettle on the fireside. The hut became warm quickly. I looked in another cupboard and found warm woollen sweaters and felt slipper boots to replace our cumbersome Innsbruckers. During all this time the German didn't speak a single word and we said only what we needed to prepare the meal. We placed the food on the table by the double windows, then by tacit understanding retired to the fireplace while the German came forward to help himself, his gun never wavering. He took a hunk of cheese and tossed it to the floor for the dog, then went back across the room balancing his open sandwich on his coffee mug. When he was seated at the other side of the hut he beckoned for us to go to the table. I have never been so hungry. After we'd eaten and the sergeant had been outside to scrub our plates in the snow, the German indicated the bench by the fire and we sat there.

The sergeant had assembled his bow and had placed it with an arrow up the back of his sweater. I had the garotte up my sleeve. Both of us knew that we were only going through the motions, as the Army manual says. This German was too wise for us, too sure of himself and his invincibility, too calm. Fear and uncertainty make a man inefficient; anger has the same effect. This man was calm; not afraid, not uncertain, not angry. I looked across the room at him; five feet ten inches, a hundred and seventy pounds and none of it fat. Hard hands used to a forester's axe or a climber's rope; a stocky compact man with good, quick reactions, yet a reservoir of thoughtful composure and calm. I put his age at no more than thirty-five, but he had the wise eyes of a man twice that age.

"Now you've eaten," he said, "and got the cold of the fjord out of your bones, we'll talk. I know you're English; now you'll tell me what you're doing here."

"First," I said, "*you* tell *me* what we are doing here. Why aren't we in the garrison at Vik or Fresvik, or at the nearest Gestapo post, which I imagine is in Voss."

He chuckled. "Let me make one thing quite clear," he said, "though I would have thought it was obvious. You are *my* prisoners, not the prisoners of the German Army. So far as I am aware the German *Army* knows nothing about you." He pointed his gun at the sergeant. "If you pull open that door, in the floor of the foyer beyond you'll find a trap door. It is very heavy but you should be able to manage it. It leads to a cellar in which you'll find a small barrel of schnapps. We may as well be comfortable."

The sergeant brought three mugs, each containing a generous portion of the fiery drink. "This is something else the German *Army* knows nothing about," the German said.

"Who the devil *are* you?" I asked. "And what do you want?"

"I want to know what is the job you have come to do."

"That doesn't answer the first part of my question. Who are you? What are you doing in these mountains with that dog? What's your name?"

"Have I asked *your* name?" he said mildly, drinking from his mug of schnapps but not taking his eyes off us for a second.

I was grateful for the raw drink; there's a kind of cold not all the fire and food will cure. I was not deceived by his amiability; I'd seen the iron in the velvet glove, knew him instinctively to be a hard man when he needed to be. If he hoped to loosen my tongue with schnapps he could think again; in the six months after I left Betty I learned to take alcohol the hard way.

"I could remind you of the Geneva Convention ..." I said.

"But you won't." His face lit with a half smile that seemed to compare us, two professionals. The sergeant was not included. He had dropped his hands behind the bench and was working the bow down, out of his sweater. Now the morning was well under way and the sun threw fan-like rays into the air behind the mountains. But it wouldn't reveal itself here on this shoulder until getting on for noon. I turned and looked out of the other window, across to the fjord. A boat was cruising slowly, its wake spreading behind it from shore to shore. "The night patrol returning to Skjolden at the tip of the fjord," the German said, looking along the line of my gaze. "Too far away to hear a few shots, and you know that's all it would take, don't you?"

Yes, I did know.

"Now tell me why have you come," he said. "I won't bother you with all that nonsense about name, rank and number. I don't care who you are and even where you have come from. I alone want to know why you are here."

"I *only* want to know, not I *alone* want to know...."

22

"Please don't try to stall for time by giving me English lessons."

"When we tell you why we are here, what then? Do you release us so we can return to England, or do you take us to the Gestapo at Voss?"

"That all depends on what you tell me, doesn't it?"

"All right. We're here to blow up the ferry boat."

"Which one?"

"Between Gudvangen and Sogndal."

"That's a lie, of course, and would you mind please telling the other man to stop what he is doing behind his back?"

"Leave it," I said, "you wouldn't stand a chance." The sergeant hastily pushed the bow back up his sweater and brought his hands round to the front, in full sight of the German. "Now back to the subject. You have not come here to blow up a ferry boat."

"The submarine depot at Larvik ... ?"

"Try again."

"The oil installations at Uskedal ... ?"

"Too far away. You'd have come in via Stavanger or the Boemlafjord. No, please, don't try my patience. You've come to do none of these things. Larvik was attacked by low-level bombers. Uskedal was unsuccessfully attacked by partisans three weeks ago, and the ferry boat's been out of action for the last week since somebody put nitric acid in the fuel tank."

I got to my feet. It was now or never. The sergeant knew it; I could hear a sharp intake of breath. The German lifted the barrel slightly so that it was aiming at my middle. I walked slowly forward, looking into his eyes the way you do a dog when you want to command without frightening it. The Labrador lifted its head and the growling started again. I held my two hands stretched out, one each side, and walked slowly forward. "Three men knew we were coming in on that rock," I said as I walked

23

across the floor. "Three men knew we'd be English when we got here. Who could have known that Larvik was attacked by low-level bombers, and that Uskedal was unsuccessfully attacked, and that somebody put nitric acid in the ferry boat unless he was either a top-rank Gestapo officer..."

Now I was within three feet of him. I leaned forward and suddenly brought in my right hand and put my thumb over the barrel of his automatic. "... Or one of the leaders of the partisans."

He put the gun aside and stood up, grinning from ear to ear. "Ragnar Bull," he said. "At your service."

"Lieutenant-Colonel Gillespie, Sergeant Milner, at *your* service."

"Don't ever do that again, sir," the sergeant said. "I damned near messed myself."

Ragnar Bull looked grave for the moment. "Passwords have become too unreliable here. We dare not trust them any more. You could have been two Germans infiltrating our partisan group, with the real colonel and sergeant trapped by the Gestapo somewhere between here and the mouth of the fjord."

"How can you be certain we are not?" the sergeant asked.

"Something your colonel said. In Britain you think Uskedal is an oil storage depot. Our attack on it failed because it was too well protected. Yesterday, while you were still on the fjord, we discovered that all they have in there is water. Plain ordinary water. Now we must find out why they use a thousand men to guard a water plant."

"But that is not the job we've come to do," I said.

"Pity, I hoped it was," Ragnar Bull said as he unclipped the magazine from his automatic.

"Do you have our stuff? It was supposed to be hidden under that rock you were standing on."

"It's in the cupboard over there; guns, ammunition,

24

explosives, rations, medical supplies. It was dropped three nights ago up on the glacier. Bjornson, my number two, sprained his ankle bringing it down. There were patrols about, so he came down the short route."

"And met a rock ...?"

"Yes."

"I thought you people invented skiing?"

"Have you ever tried it with a hundred-and-fifty-pound pack on your back?"

"He was lucky. There are detonators and guncotton among that stuff."

"He knew that; but you can't stop Bjornson when he sets his mind to something. He's a fisherman from the north, from Narvik; he was born on a trawler at sea. You'll meet him tomorrow. He'll get a surprise when he finds you here."

"He doesn't know?"

"Nobody knows but me, and Knut Kierulf, and ..."

His words were cut off by a burst of machine-gun fire that came in through the window and chopped through his chest. A dancing spray brought bubbles of foam flecked with blood as he smashed back against the table and sprawled half over it. There was no doubt that he was dead. His dog growled, then fell when a bullet smashed its head. I was paralysed by the shock but the sergeant major chopped my legs behind the knees and brought me down, thrust the automatic and its magazine at me, and scuttled across the floor to the cupboard. There seemed to be ten machine-guns all pouring fire through that window and the woodwork was riddled with bullets. Thank God there was stone only at the fireplace: the ricochets whanged across the room like twanged piano wires. Sergeant Milner had pulled open the door of the cupboard and found a haversack which fortunately the partisans had opened. He dragged a waxed cardboard box beneath the window and cursed as he pulled it open. It

25

was filled with loaded magazines. There was also a Thompson machine-gun; he clipped a magazine to it, and lay there, waiting. I had crawled across the floor to lie beside him; still the shooting continued, a hell house of banging bullets that crackled in the air. The base of the wooden wall was a solid log but still we heard the shots from outside thudding against it. "They're fifty yards away," he said, but I had to lip-read to catch the words, so constant was the fusillade.

"Germans?" I mouthed.

"A patrol?"

"Why would they shoot?"

At that moment a stick grenade came in the window. The sergeant grabbed it and threw it underarm through the other window. We could hear other stick bombs hit the outside of the hut and clatter to the ground, and we waited what seemed like an eternity, though it could only have been a second before they exploded. The log took most of the impact and shifted inwards slightly. The window frame buckled and the glass flew in all directions. Just then the bomb we had thrown out exploded on the other side and more glass came hurtling in. I felt three cuts on my cheek, wiped my hand across my face and came away with blood. The sergeant was unharmed. So far.

The firing stopped. "Come on," I said, and ran on all fours across to the inside door of the foyer. It was studded with holes. Several bullets had hit the catch and the hinges, but I managed to drag it open. They'd be sending men round the sides of the hut and would hold their fire. I reached into the cupboard and found a slab of guncotton. I tore open a tin box of detonators, slipped one inside the guncotton, crimped it on the end of a piece of fuse pre-cut to twelve inches, just as I'd requested in my stores indent. Outside that door was the wooden hatch. I lifted it. It was heavy. In the small cellar beneath the hut was stored extra food, logs, schnapps, even a five-gallon can of paraffin. I dragged the paraffin up and rolled it across the floor towards the stone hearth.

"I think they're coming again," he said.

I struck a fuse match and set it to the end of the fuse. At first I thought it was going out and cursed it, but then the fuse caught and started its acrid splutter. I handed the slab of guncotton to Sergeant Milner, and he put it on the hearth near the can of paraffin. Then we crawled down the cellar and dropped the heavy wooden trap door into its sealing rim above us. It was a good fit, thick timber, carpenter-crafted, and well braced. It would need to be. I was counting silently. So was the sergeant, and I could hear him in the darkness. I wanted to scrabble out of that hole and run, the way I always wanted to run when the explosives were set and the fuse was burning. Each second of a burning fuse occupies a lifetime in the minds of those who wait for the bang, but there was nothing we could do about it. Except wait. We crouched in the dark cellar amidst the logs and the tubs of brisling and the wheels of cotton-wrapped cheese that smelled of summer and sunshine, and the barrels of apples. We put a finger in each ear trumpet, compressed our nostrils with the palms of our hands and closed our mouths tightly, lips clenched. I even tightened the cheeks of my arse. And counted, and waited.

Guncotton is issued in slabs eight inches by four by three. You can hit it with a rifle butt, fire bullets into it, chop it with an axe, nail it to a cross, and it doesn't explode. You can wear it on your back when you jump and even if your parachute doesn't open the guncotton will go into the ground with you without exploding—not that that's much of a consolation, but at least there's enough of you left to dig up and bury. You can carry guncotton in the heat of your crotch without fear of losing your manhood; you can shred it with a knife and it'll burn slowly enough

27

to brew a cup of tea/sugar/milk substitute. Some say you can nibble it when you're constipated, but I never tried that. Each block has a hole in the centre into which you put an explosive plug containing a detonator; when that plug goes off it takes the guncotton with it. One slab expands into an enormous volume of gas that has to find an outlet somewhere and will devastate anything in its path. It'll slice a railway line neat as a wire cuts cheese, it'll pulverise bricks and masonry and puff down a wall as if it belonged to a doll's house, it'll flick a roof into the air like an opened jack-in-a-box.

That slab of guncotton I'd slid across the floor upstairs could explode only upwards and outwards, bursting the can of paraffin and spraying its contents in a raging torrent of flame. The other slabs that were stored in the cupboard would blow too, and create a holocaust above our heads that would shatter the walls and roof of that hut.

Or, if the baulks above the cellar were not strong enough, the blast would come down and scour the pit in which we were crouched.

The world exploded above us, and my heart rang with an almighty thump that seemed to bang every part of my body at the same time, and I knew my nose was bleeding and my ears were blocked and my throat had flooded with bilious vomit and my bladder had emptied itself and all the air was roaring with noise and crackling flame and my senses reeled and I slumped to the floor, sliding boneless onto the earth. But when I opened my eyes, I was still alive, and the sergeant on the floor beside me was alive too. I spat the vomit out of my mouth and wiped my face with my sleeve. He wiped his face, looked at the back of his hand and saw the blood which seeped from one nostril. The crackle of flames above us sounded like machine-gun fire; three beams of light flickered down through cracks the explosion had sprung in the trap door; but we were still alive. Smoke and dancing dust particles

28

came down the light beams, and while we cleaned our faces the flames died down. No doubt the paraffin had scattered and only a small quantity had flared on the floor above us. The walls would have been blown outwards; the roof would first lift, then crash down, burying us in a pile of debris and splintered wood. But we were still alive.

We waited. There were no sounds, no footsteps, nobody trying to shift the rubble. No one could possible believe that we were still alive after such an explosion. There had been ten blocks of guncotton and two boxes of detonators in that cupboard, and I had once derailed a seven-coach ammunition train with five blocks.

"All we have to do now, sir," the sergeant said, "is wait until they go home and dig ourselves out."

"If any of them is still alive after a bang like that."

Both of us were covered in fine dust. The sergeant started to brush my uniform, tut-tutting as if I were improperly dressed for a palace reception. He took a handkerchief from his pocket. God knows why it had stayed so impeccable. He turned the tap on the schnapps cask, wet the handkerchief, and handed it to me. I wiped my face, grateful for the tingle it brought to my skin. When I had finished, he held out an apple, peeled and cored and ready to eat.

"Here you are, sir. Eat this," he said. "It'll take the dust out of your throat."

"I could use a drink of that schnapps."

"The apple will be better for you, if you don't mind my saying so, sir."

We stayed in the cellar all day. Late in the afternoon a German ski patrol came past, poked in a desultory fashion among the timber and left. By that time we had opened the hatch a half an inch to give ourselves more air. The hinges appeared to be undamaged, we'd have no difficulty when we chose to climb out.

Shortly after dark we heard scuttling among the timbers. It was a timber wolf attracted by the scent of the blood and exploded flesh and bone. I clicked the bolt on the gun I'd taken into the cellar with me. It was an old familiar sound to him and he ran away.

About ten o'clock a group came silently as if from nowhere. "Ragnar," one of them called softly, "Ragnar . . . ?"

I beckoned the sergeant to stand back against the wall and squatted behind the schnapps cask where any light from the hatch would not immediately find me. A lot of scraping noise as timber was dragged away and then the hatch was lifted. "Ragnar," the voice called again, and I saw the light of a torch shining into the cellar.

We stayed still, not even breathing.

Take a chance? I'd moved too soon once before; could I afford to take a chance now? These were Norwegians, certainly; no German could fake the Norwegian accent as accurately as the man who called for Ragnar.

"Knut Kierulf?" I called cautiously. "Bjornson?"

"Who's down there?" the deep voice asked in Riksmaal Norwegian. "Where is Ragnar Bull?"

"Dead. He was caught by the first machine-gun."

"But you escaped?"

"Yes."

"What happened to Ragnar's dog?"

"It was killed too. We blew up the hut. You won't find any traces of Ragnar or his dog, I'm afraid."

"Say something in English."

"Bjornson is a fisherman from Narvik, and he was born at sea on a trawler."

The deep voice boomed in a grim laugh. "All right," he said, "come up. Only Ragnar would have told you such rubbish as that."

We climbed out of the cellar, slamming the hatch. "You've had other visitors today," the deep voice said behind us.

30

Three of them, one a girl, all in white parkas and trousers. One had a large pistol which he pointed at my stomach. "Which is Bjornson?" I asked.

The man with the pistol looked at the other two. "I am," he said.

"And this is Knut Kierulf . . . ?" I asked.

"It's not Edvard Grieg, though he could have been if the Germans hadn't come."

The girl stepped forward. "I'm Aud," she said, "and Ragnar Bull was my father's brother. You saw him shot?"

I nodded. There were tears in her eyes, but she was not crying. "If it helps you," I said, "he died very quickly."

"We live for that, here in Norway," she said, "to die quickly. The Germans don't like us. We don't bend the knee to them like some of the other countries."

"My name is Gillespie," I said, "Donald Gillespie. And this is Sergeant Milner."

"And you must be freezing to death."

"No, I have this sweater."

"I recognised it. It belongs to my uncle."

Bjornson put his arm round her shoulder. "We have a long way to go, Aud," he said.

I looked at our feet with dismay. Our Innsbruckers had been blown to pieces in the explosion, and we had only those felt slipper boots that wouldn't last a mile in snow. "Put your feet on my skis behind mine," Bjornson said, "and hold me round the waist."

"I thought you had sprained your ankle?"

"That was days ago. Hold on tight."

"And close your eyes," Aud said laughing. "Bjornson's the fastest man you'll ever ride behind."

We went pick-a-back down the mountainside, doing all the movements I'd practised so many times but faster than I'd ever imagined possible and with an unconscious grace and verve that took my breath away. Sergeant Milner rode behind Knut, and Aud weaved patterns behind us, guarding our rear but ready should anyone take a tumble. Half-way along a traverse we stopped to let the others catch us.

"You ski well," Bjornson said, "for a man who'd use the Austrian method if I'd let him ..."

We travelled eight miles along slopes that gradually descended from the glacier to a second hut; this time, however, Aud and Bjornson guarded the outside while Knut and the sergeant and I went inside to find white parkas, hoods, trousers, ski boots, skis and poles.

We arrived at Loftheim by four o'clock in the morning. Even after such a short time with these people, I felt as if I knew each one of them well; I had already established a tentative rapport with them. I could see they were proud and courageous, each in his or her own way; collectively they would make a close-locked deadly striking force. Already I trusted them; when they told me the house in Loftheim where we were to stay was safe, I climbed beneath a goose-feather quilt and was asleep within five minutes.

Loftheim is a village of wooden houses south of Voss overlooking the Hardangerfjord. Only four hundred people lived there; most of the men had either fled to England or been taken by the Germans. Before the war the principal occupations in the village were farming, timber-cutting, and tourism. The village had one of the best preserved Stave churches for many miles around, and several good hotels used in summer by walkers and in winter by skiers. When the Germans commandeered the herds the dairy farming came to an end. The soil around the village is rocky and not suitable for arable farming. The farms are small, none more than twenty-five acres, and they struggle to grow a mixed crop of potatoes, barley and oats. Some small dessert apples grow on the south slopes—as if to compensate for the difficulties, the apples though small are incredibly sweet.

Life in the village has always been hard and would have been impossible were it not for the discovery in 1926 of titanium on the banks of a small fjord about two miles north of Loftheim, a small but rich find of ilmenite which gave employment to any of the village men who cared to work there. It was difficult for most of them to come in off the clean hillside saeters and go down into a dirty mine; that many managed to do it was a tribute to their courage and a testimony to the rigours of hill-farming on land in which few things but trees will grow.

No garrison was permanently stationed in Loftheim since the village itself had no strategic importance. It was, however, on the 'training' circuit, and small German units would move in from time to time, always without warning. Then the patrols would start, the sudden movements under the pretext of manoeuvres. It was not safe to be out at night, or to have food on your table, or drink, or to carry a sharpened knife in your pocket or a woodsman's axe at your belt, lest the Germans accuse you of bearing an offensive weapon.

These visits were infrequent, and the village was left alone most of the time. The villagers carried on more or less as they had always done though the shops had little to sell, the tourist hotels were empty, and the cable cars from the Hardanger fjord no longer ran. Most people stayed in their homes and farmhouses, keeping themselves aloof since it was hard to know whom to trust, and settled down to the grim struggle for survival. Occasionally in the late afternoons, the women would walk to the houses of those they knew well and sit for an hour gossiping quietly, mending clothing they could not replace, unravelling old woollen garments and knitting them again. They would sip substitute coffee with wry smiles, broach illicit bottles of schnapps, and wait to be told if their menfolk were among the dead.

The titanium mine had been taken over by the Germans and was being worked with Lithuanian forced labour who were housed in a hastily constructed prison compound near the minehead. The Norwegian miners from Loftheim and Ulskeid refused to work the mine until the Germans began killing their wives and children. Early in 1941 the women held a meeting at which they decided to stop the mine work, despite the Germans. The men blew up the mine shaft, then took to the mountains. Some escaped to England and joined the Norwegian Army under King Haakon; others went over the border into Sweden and the underground training battalions; others stayed in hiding in the hills, refusing to leave the homeland. With the men gone, and all the able-bodied women in hiding, the Germans forbore to take reprisals. Knut Kierulf was mayor of Loftheim and stayed at his post. Some said it was his influence and eloquence that prevented a bloody massacre.

For whatever reasons, the Germans permitted life in Loftheim to resume its normal pace, and brought the Lithuanians to clear and work the mine. The Norwegians were shocked when they saw the first forced-labour gangs arrive at Voss. Most of them had been 'liberated' from Russian prison camps and, though they were starved and beaten, they had been put back to work in conditions more appalling than even the Russians could contrive. Local partisans helped several prisoners to escape, but they all died before they could reach the Swedish border. They were too weak, too emaciated, too tired to travel clandestinely across open snow-packed country. After a while, the Norwegians saw there was nothing they could do to help them, and left the Lithuanians to work and die in peace.

One by one, the women came back from the mountains; one by one houses that had been abandoned were opened again, fires were lighted and the soft glow of lamps warmed the streets of the village. The German patrols still came from time to time, but they left the people alone. Knut Kierulf tried the experiment of inviting the German officers into his house whenever they were stationed in the village. He'd call in a few of his older friends and they'd spend an evening looking for subjects of conversation. Despite the difficulties, Knut persisted and his attitude paid dividends. The villagers became much less suspect to the Germans, much less likely to have their houses searched. Gradually Loftheim acquired a friendly reputation among the Germans, and some of the men came home from the mountains and resumed their farming. The telegraph exchange was re-opened under German supervision, and the generating plant and the sewage

35

works were started again. It would have taken fifteen or twenty thousand troops to police the area effectively. The garrison commander concentrated on making the mine impregnable and left the outlying stabburs to the mercies of mobile squads whose instructions were simple and explicit: look for trouble, cure it, and don't take prisoners. In the first three months of operation the mobile death squads, as they were called, blew up or burned down five stabburs and killed an estimated thirty Norwegians. Five Germans were killed in an ambush mounted by children and old women.

The sergeant and I were housed in the home of two of the partisans, Per Vidgren and his wife Kari. It stood on the edge of Loftheim on the Ulskeid road in a quarter acre of birch, ash, beech, and oak. Before the war Per's father had been one of the mine engineers; the first of the rebels, he had been killed in 1940. Kari had an amazing ability— she was the only person I ever met who could put her hip joints out at will. In this way she had avoided the fate of many young Norwegian girls of being sent to the forced labour and other camps in Germany. She never left the house through the front gate except with both her hips out of joint and in a self-propelled wheel chair; when she left by the back she could move faster and more silently than a mountain deer. She was a pretty girl, tall and lissom from a life spent out of doors; with her hips out, however, she hobbled in a horribly ungainly manner and further degraded her appearance by tucking her golden hair into an unattractive bun, and wearing steel-rimmed glasses which made her squint.

Per Vidgren went into the mountains with the others in 1941, but he didn't go to England. Occasionally he'd come down to see Kari; gradually he formed the habit of staying the night, and now lived there all the time, avoiding the windows and hiding in the timber when anyone came to the house. This was the way most of the partisans lived;

36

they had the wary eyes of hunted animals, constantly flicking backwards and forwards, side to side, trusting nothing and nobody, agile, nimble and cautious.

That first evening they came through the timber at the back of Per's house like a gathering of wolves: Aud Bull, the niece of Ragnar, Knut Kierulf and Bjornson the man from Narvik, Tor and Ola from Ulskeid, Astrid from the stabbur I could see from Per's loft window, Anne from farther along the valley. At my request the sergeant was absent.

Anne brought a bottle of schnapps her mother had distilled. We all drank from the bottle so as to leave no tell-tale glasses should we need to decamp in a hurry. Mostly they squatted on the floor around Bjornson, Aud, and Knut, who sat at a table at one end of the room. I sat on a bench covered with a cretonne cushion wide enough to sleep on and tucked under the gable window which was covered by curtains of hand-made lace. The same lace covered all the windows of this house. I looked round the room, suddenly aware that our relative positions were those of a court with me in a witness box, their eminences on the bench, and the tribunal in a neat half-circle. When the schnapps bottle had finished its second round Knut coughed and called the meeting to order.

"We all know about Ragnar," he said, "but we've seen too many of our people die in that way to want to mourn them anywhere but in our hearts and our memories. If any of us can get to church, we can bend the knee and say a few words to the pastor, and Ola will inscribe his name on the tile." He looked up at me. "For the benefit of our English friend I'll explain that our roll of honour is kept on a tile in the roof of a church; after the war it will be suitably blessed in our church here in Loftheim, and mounted in a place of honour, so that our children and our children's children and Norwegians throughout

37

all of time will remember the infamy of the German nation."

I nodded, as if I understood. But how could I? My country had not been invaded, my people had not been murdered and raped and tortured and plundered as these people had. They were simple Evangelical Lutherans; faith was strong in them and uncomplicated by dogma and ritual; from this tap root into the purpose of life itself they derived their enormous strength and courage. This meeting was the requiem for Ragnar; he'd need no other until the Germans had been pushed out of his country.

Everyone seemed to be watching Aud Bull, and she was looking at me in a contemplative sort of way. "My uncle said nothing to us about your arrival," she said after Knut had finished. "We have checked the boats in which you came, and they were as you said. We knew about the drop, of course. Bjornson and I went up the mountain to bring the material down into the hut, but that was only because my uncle told us to go. He did not tell us *why* there was to be a drop."

"Did no-one else know I was coming?" I asked, looking round. Everybody was looking at everybody else.

"Who operates the radio?"

"My uncle operated it, alone."

"And no-one else knew I was coming?"

Knut Kierulf looked at me. I remembered what Ragnar had said as the machine-gun bullets hit him. "Bjornson will get a surprise when he finds you here. Nobody knows but me, and Knut Kierulf, and ..." That was the moment at which the bullets had struck him. I avoided looking at Knut Kierulf. If he had anything to say, let him say it without prompting from me. If he said nothing, I damned well wanted to know why. It may have been an accident, the mobile death squad's coming to the hut, but then again, they may have been forewarned. It was surely unusual, even for the mobile death squad, to pump

38

machine-gun bullets into a building without searching it first.

"I knew the Englishmen were coming," Knut said. "Ragnar told me before he left for the rendezvous."

"There wasn't supposed to be a rendezvous," I said.

"I mean, before he left to transfer the equipment from the hut to the rock."

"So you knew about the rock? Did you know about the rock, Bjornson; and you, Miss Bull, did you know about the rock?"

Both shook their heads, puzzled.

"Bjornson was second-in-command, I believe?" I said, again looking round. I didn't want a dialogue with Knut; I wanted them all to ask the questions I was asking. If Bjornson was the second-in-command, why did Ragnar tell Knut and not Bjornson about my arrival? And if he told Knut, whom else did he tell? And why wasn't that other person speaking out? I'd been told in England that only three people knew I was coming, and they had been described as 'unimpeachable'. The partisans had weeded out all the quislings by now, or so we thought. So how did the mobile death squad get on to us so quickly? Surely the Gestapo would have been interested in talking to me, if only to learn why I had come. No-one knew, of that I was certain. Not even Sergeant Milner knew that, which is why I had specifically excluded him from this meeting.

"I didn't know about the rock," Bjornson said, "and I don't think Aud knew."

"No, I didn't know," she said. "My uncle believed people should only be told what they needed to know. He obviously didn't intend anyone else to meet you, and so he told no-one."

"Then why did he tell Knut? Knut didn't need to know. There was to be no rendezvous, not there by the fjord. We were to contact you later, in another place."

39

"Ragnar didn't tell me deliberately," Knut said. "I was with him by chance when the message came through. I don't suppose he meant to tell me but since I happened to be there I guess he didn't see any reason why he shouldn't tell me."

"Look here," Bjornson said, "why have you come? We haven't planned a job; we didn't send for you." He looked around the group, drawing support from them. Now I was the one in the dock, the intrusive, unwanted stranger.

"That titanium mine," I said. "We want it stopped. That titanium is too valuable to the German war effort."

Per was a slow-thinking person. He was sitting on the floor beside Kari. He got up and walked slowly around the room. "I don't understand," he said. "If you wanted the titanium stopped, why didn't you send us a message? We could have stopped it. Or if you didn't trust us to do the job, why didn't you drop a force by parachute? You have enough Norwegians in London who know this part of the world; they could have done something about the mine. Anyway, the best place to attack the mine is not in the mine itself. We've discussed this several times and we're all agreed. Let them mine the ore; it keeps a garrison occupied just guarding the Lithuanians, for example. Let them guard the ore convoys to the treatment plant at Granvin; but when the metal comes out of Granvin, one lorry load for a week's output, that's the time to attack. But we've discussed this over and over again, and we're all agreed."

"Despite the fact that the metal is best guarded when they bring it from Granvin?"

"We've taken that into account."

I was trying to say it would be a suicide mission; but obviously they knew that. "We still think the mine ought to be stopped," I said, "and I've come to try to work out the best way to do it." That would hold them as a cover story; it would account for my presence in the district for as long as I needed to stay.

"And the other man, your sergeant?" Ola asked.

"He has an old score to settle. His mother was Norwegian; the Germans killed her, in Oslo. She was parachuted early in 1941. She was fifty-five and the medical officers said she'd never make it; she proved them all wrong."

"But she was taken and killed?"

"She was betrayed. I wouldn't like to be the person who gave her away when the sergeant gets hold of him!"

Sergeant Milner was sitting under a pine tree at the northernmost edge of the timber behind Per Vidgren's house.

"Hello, Bill," I said.

"Hello, Colonel. How did the meeting go?"

"As well as could be expected. I planted the story about your mother in Oslo."

"If ever she gets to hear of it, she'll flay me alive."

"Harrogate's a long way away. Anyway, she'd like the embroidery. I said she parachuted in against medical advice at fifty-five!"

"She'd like that. When are you going to finish my briefing, Colonel?"

Poor bugger didn't know what it was all about, though we'd studied the ground together from aerial photographs back at the briefing centre in Maida Vale. He knew the topography and the people, but that was about all.

"Not yet. It was bad enough to bring you along as a decoy without running the risk that you'll have something to tell them if they catch you."

"I *did* volunteer, Colonel," he reminded me, gently.

He was wearing off-white woollen trousers, boots with the fur turned outwards, a white silk anorak over a thick woollen sweater, and a knitted woollen hat with a bobble on it. He stood up, five feet ten of solid bone and muscle. He was my batman, back in England, and though he made my bed and served my meals and poured my wine, he was as tough as an old saddle. He'd need to be; the briefings I'd had for this job were the worst ever, and I'd had some bad ones in my time.

People get the wrong idea of a briefing; they think you go into a room full of knowledgeable boffins each of whom, an expert in his field, has prepared himself to tell you everything you need to know. All specialists. We'd been briefed by a committee that I wouldn't trust to decide the siting of the next public lavatory. Granted any job in Norway was confused by the situation of the Norwegian government-in-exile, who had decreed that partisan activity be kept to a minimum. The order was peaceful non-co-operation. Too many Norwegians had been shot when the Germans first arrived; too much of Norway's scant industry had been destroyed by indiscriminate sabotage. The government-in-exile was looking to the future, when the war was over. The fishing fleet had escaped and was now earning immense revenue under charter. Taking the wider view, the government saw no purpose in killing a sentry here or blowing up a railway bridge there. Thus any job such as ours was suspect and the Allied High Command would grant permission for it only with reluctance.

The committee that briefed me had met more difficulties than most, I suppose, being charitable, but I resented the way in which my sergeant had been allowed to stick his neck out on so little information. How much could I tell him? I was under orders, of course, to tell him only what he needed to know for his own safety and the success of the job. I truly believed that the less he knew, the better for him. Even Gestapo interrogators stop when they realise you've nothing to tell them and fling you into a camp or give you a quick easy death. It's impossible to convince them you know nothing if you've been fully briefed; they're far too clever, far too professional. But was I being fair to this man by not taking him into my confidence, by not seeking the benefit of his advice? After all, I had a double

43

responsibility to him; he was not only one of my troops but he had served me personally as a batman. He'd looked after my possessions but more than that, he'd cared for *me* for more than a year on several jobs and between jobs.

"This isn't neat and tidy, Bill. Not like the time we dropped into Carrara."

"You can say that again, Colonel."

"I'm groping in the dark most of the time."

"I rather gathered that."

"Trust me, will you?"

"I just don't want to let you down, Colonel."

"You won't ..."

He was ideally suited to this job, though I couldn't tell him so without telling him what the job was. He had all the qualifications: at ten yards he could split a card side on with a bullet, a knife, or an arrow fired from a steel bow; he could go up rocks like a mountain goat and still be fit to fight at the top; he could blow a rail or a bridge's footings with the minimum of noise and the maximum of blast; he could cross a field so silently that a rabbit would sit licking its paws while he passed by. And he could cook—M and V stew with added biscuits turned to best broth of beef in his mess tin; chicken-in-the-bucket and baked river fish were his specialities.

He played a trombone in England. Dorsey style. We hadn't brought the trombone with us. Not on this job. This was a tough one. Aud, Knut, Bjornson, Per, Tor, and Ola; Anne, Kari, and Astrid. All good Norwegians. One of them was a quisling and it was my job to find out which. And then to kill him. Or her. The sergeant was supposed to flush out the traitor while I watched, guarding his rear. But I couldn't tell him that, or so I'd been informed. However, I'd have to tell him about the other jobs we'd come to do.

"You remember the aerial photographs of the mine?"

"Yes, sir. I think I've got it fixed in my mind."

"Good. We're going to knock it out of action."

"What about the Lithuanians?"

"That's job number two. We are going to try to release them."

"We'll lose a lot, sir. The reports say they're in no condition to travel. Not our way ..."

"Twenty a month are dying anyway. The Germans don't bother to feed them properly, since it's easier to send more workers than to arrange for a regular decent supply of food."

He was silent for a moment; then he sat down again, squatting on his hunkers beneath the tree.

"What do the partisans think?" he asked.

"They'd rather steer clear of the mine itself and get the metal when it comes out of the processing plant. That way, they can hide the metal for use after the war at the same time as they frustrate the Germans."

"It makes sense."

"Twenty people dying every month doesn't make sense."

He nodded his head. Like me, he didn't give a damn about titanium stored until after the war. The Lithuanians were dying here and now.

"How shall we do the job, sir? Alone? With the partisans?" He smiled. "Or shall we ask them back in England to drop a parachute division?"

"Ever hopeful. This job, I'll grant you, needs two thousand men."

"But you think we can do it with two?"

"That's what I hope."

"You'll be talking to England, won't you, Colonel?"

I nodded.

"Then ask them to send your other pair of boots. You'll ruin your feet wearing those things."

"When are you going to stop being a batman?"

He smiled again. "When you learn to look after yourself, sir," he said.

*   *   *

I spent three days hiding in a snow burrow in the mountains, watching the routine of the mine, the German camp, and the prisoners' compound. Sergeant Milner stayed in Per Vidgren's house and came to visit me each night shortly before dawn. Each time, he reported, someone had set out to follow him.

"But you haven't identified them yet?"

"Acting on your instructions, sir, I haven't tried. I've concentrated on giving them the slip so as not to lead them here."

"Do you think they know where I am?"

"No, sir. I'm certain they don't know."

I was confident no-one would take a crack at him until the quisling knew more about our plans.

The mine was situated at the edge of a small fjord south-west of Voss, and a rail link had been constructed between there and the village of Bulken, on the main line between Voss and Bergen. A spur line connected Voss with Granvin. The ore trains were always accompanied by flat cars carrying soldiers and a mounted Spandau. Two soldiers rode in front of the engine and two at the back of the train on what must have been the world's coldest railway ride. The ore trains never travelled at more than ten miles an hour; the unfortunate two men at the front spent the entire journey lying flat, examining every inch of the line as the train moved along, looking for explosives, cut sections, pressure mines. Riding the train in that position was used as a punishment; in the early days it had often been a death sentence.

The mine itself went back into the rock, not down into the ground, and the gallery entrance was as high and vaulted as a small cathedral. Four administrative buildings crouched round the minehead as if to keep out of the bitter wind that swept down the mountainside and over the fjord, carrying with it the smoke and stench from the diesel generating plant that provided light and ran the electric trains to haul the ore trucks in and out. The German workers always scuttled between the buildings clutching their coats and parkas around them. Only the Lithuanian forced workers walked, shuffling forward like pensioners going to a comrade's funeral.

They lived in a compound a quarter of a mile from the mine, four rows of tin huts surrounded by a double barbed wire perimeter that ended in the fjord itself. They wore black woollen trousers, grey shirts and black jackets; their hair had been shorn, men and women alike, and a stripe shaved two inches wide from brow to nape. Any skin wound was treated by splashing the area with a violet solution kept in a bucket near the entrance to the compound; it stained their skin with the only colour in a white, grey, and black life.

The shifts were changed twice a day, at eight in the morning and eight at night. First the mine was cleared. Then four German soldiers went in with dogs. When they had come out the others were allowed in. The two shifts passed on the road from the compound with no sign of recognition, no greetings.

While I watched through my binoculars, three corpses were thrown into an uncovered lime-pit, and almost at the same time a lorry-load of reinforcements arrived. They were pushed off the back of the lorry at the entrance to the compound. No-one appeared to tell them what to do, and gradually they found places for themselves in the huts. There were no names, no roll calls, no identification parades. Once in this compound, they ceased to exist, their only exit the road to and from the mine or the uncovered lime-pit.

The Germans guarding the prisoners lived in comparative luxury in a wooden camp on the other side of the mine, with showers, lavatories, and a camp mess hut from which after dark I could hear music and, one night, a film show; they appeared to ignore the Lithuanians entirely. Four mounted guard outside the prisoners' compound; they never risked going inside except for the search and the twice-daily soup and bread distribution. Nor did I see any prisoners go into the German compound, not even to perform menial camp tasks; I guessed they carried a load of lice the Germans could well do without.

The officers appeared to spend as little time in the camp as possible. They had an Officers' Mess in what must have been a pension hotel near the mine, with living quarters in the rooms above. A Commandant, a man I took to be his Adjutant, one officer who scurried about with a clip-board and wore the worried look of administration, and, of course, a Medical Officer. I never saw the M.O. go into the prisoners' compound; they were obviously not in his charge. Every morning a sick parade of German soldiers waited outside his hut.

He was a good doctor and, surprisingly, an efficient soldier. I learned that when I took the Commando Hardening Course with him at Achnacarry, in Scotland.

He was a plant.

A true Aryan German, he was born in Hamburg of impeccably German parentage. His father became manager of the Danish subsidiary of a food importing company, and the family lived in Denmark for many years. The boy was brought up with almost dual nationality. When he was old enough, he was sent back to Göttingen University, where he obtained a degree in medicine. Then he went to England and held an internship at Guy's Hospital. There he added English to the Danish and German he already spoke. In 1940 he took part in the invasion of Denmark as a medical officer of the Wehrmacht, but he was cap-

48

tured and brought to England. He told me his story the last time I saw him.

"When I arrived in England," Klaus said, "I told them I was a qualified doctor and offered my services in the P.O.W. camp near Kettering. One of my fellow prisoners had a ruptured appendix and I operated on him as an emergency case. Afterwards, he was sent to hospital, where the surgeon asked to see me to congratulate me on what I'd done. It had been a sharp penknife and boiling water job. The surgeon turned out to be one of my former professors at Guy's. I talked with him, quite frankly, about my attitudes, and shortly after that was taken to London, under escort of course, to a house in Maida Vale."

I knew the house, and the brigadier who'd interviewed Klaus when he got there. The same brigadier had briefed me for this Norway job.

"I was examined at great length by psychiatrists and psychologists," Klaus said to me, "and eventually they must have decided that I wasn't insane, wasn't lying, and really did hate the Germans, despite being born one myself. Look, I was brought up in Denmark; I was as much Danish as German. I had many Danish friends, spoke their language as fluently as I did my own. How could I forgive what the Germans were doing to them? Anyway, the Brigadier finally asked me to work for Special Services and I agreed. They gave me a cover story, and I acted it out by 'escaping' from a prisoner-of-war camp in Yorkshire. It was a real escape with another prisoner, and I was almost shot. He was recaptured.

"From there I made my way to a bomber aerodrome in Suffolk. You'd be amazed how easy it was. I went by train. No-one suspected me, since I'd 'stolen' a blue uniform with a white shirt and red tie that the sick soldiers wear. Everyone was most kind and bought me food and cups of tea and treated me like a hero. My plan had been to get to the coast and somehow steal a boat. When I

49

heard two airmen talking on the train, I changed my mind, and decided to go the quick way, by air. The two airmen flew in Stirling bombers, which travelled low enough for me not to need oxygen. They also contain a bed—one of the airmen had lost his cigarette lighter and it had rolled under the bed, he said, and wasn't found for five trips. I listened to everything the airmen said, and got off the train when they did. How did I find the aerodrome? I took a taxi, and paid him off outside the camp. It was so simple, I've often wondered how the Royal Air Force ever managed to fly. The security at that aerodrome was non-existent. I walked into the camp through an unguarded gate that led to the actual air field. Once inside the camp, I spent about half an hour just walking around. I was never challenged. I went into an office. It wasn't even locked. I removed a bundle of papers and carried them in my hand. Next stop a large shed, from which I removed a parachute, a parachute harness, and an airman's leather flying helmet with earphones. Then I walked out across the field to where the Stirling planes were waiting, already loaded with petrol and bombs, climbed aboard one of them, and hid myself under the bed, wearing the parachute harness and the flying helmet, but stowing the parachute under the bed to help conceal me. When the crew came aboard, nobody looked under the bed, and the plane took off a short time later. I plugged the flying helmet into the intercommunication system, and listened to the pilot talking to his crew.

"My God, the plane was cold, and I almost froze.

"The target, I learned on the intercom, was to be Dusseldorf. The navigator gave them all a warning when we were fifteen minutes from the area, and I slipped out from under the bed and put on my parachute. The nearest crew member, the wireless operator, was sitting forward from me, facing his set. The interior of the plane was pitch black, with each position faintly illuminated. Another airman sat in the forward end of the plane writing on an official looking pad; he bent his head close to the paper in the dim red cock-pit light.

"I went aft, past the mid-upper turret, which was slowly rotating from left to right and back again. The gunner had eyes only for the night sky outside, astern of the aircraft and above it, searching for fighters. Through the turret I could see the night sky, though there was little moon. I inched my way forward. The gunner did not so much as glance inside the plane. Since the engines were making such a noise, I knew there was no chance he'd hear me, but I found myself moving on tip-toe anyway. Further aft, I came to a couple of steps leading down to the fuselage floor, with the rear gunner a little further along, also rotating his turret and scanning the sky behind and below us. Near the gunner was an escape hatch in the floor, supported by four clamps. It was hearing a story from one of the airmen in the train, about an escape hatch blowing open, that had made me decide to make the trip by plane. When I realised, however, how close the gunner was, I doubted if I could get the hatch open without attracting his attention. Through his plastic 'bubble' I could see the sky again, and reflections of searchlights from the ground as they sought the other planes in the squadron. I could hear explosions below us, but felt no shudder in the plane.

"I stepped slowly forward, inch by inch. The gunner continued his search of the sky, his hand resting on the firing mechanism of the gun. I'd unplugged my earphones when I left the space under the bed; I longed to be wearing them, if only to hear if I had been spotted and some flight engineer was creeping behind me through the darkness with a spanner in his hand. I stood beside the escape hatch and bent down. Parachute harness tight. Parachute clipped to it, quite secure. Handle on the right side, ready to pull after a count of ten. I unfastened one clamp, reached

51

across and quickly unfastened the one opposite and the
one to the left. Only one to go. Watch the gunner, slowly
traversing. You'd think he'd *have known* I was there
wouldn't you, but if he did, he made no sign. Last clamp
unfastened, and then a quick pull upwards and to the
side and the escape hatch came up and I put it to one side
and felt the sudden rush of ice cold air coming into the
plane. I knew the gunner would feel it too. I wanted to
jump instantly, but I hadn't screwed up my nerve. Then
I looked back and the rear gunner had turned round and
I could see his lips move in a shout and his hand left the
gun and went into his pocket where he probably had a
knife or a pistol, and then I heaved my buttocks off the
edge of the hole and the slipstream took me out and
down, dropping towards Germany.

"It was a dry night, with no rain. I made a textbook
landing and the guards of an artillery camp took me
prisoner within minutes. They'd watched me coming down.

"Then they sent out a lorry from Ottenhagen, and I
was taken to the Gestapo headquarters. From there they
sent me, again by lorry, to Hamburg. That was a stroke
of luck for me. I was born in Hamburg. Only my intimate
knowledge of the city and the indisputable identification
of my father convinced the Gestapo that my incredible
story of being an escaped prisoner-of-war was true. The
papers I'd stolen from the R.A.F. helped."

Klaus had told me this story in France, when he'd
helped me rescue a man we wanted from a hospital in
Rouen. The Germans were carrying out genetic and other
monstrous experiments, and we blew the hospital staff
quarters, and the entire pack of sadistic butchering sur-
geons, sky high. Now he was working for us in Norway,
and I hoped none of the partisans knew of his existence.
Not even Sergeant Milner had been told.

Klaus was my ace-in-the-hole.

"What happened to you in Hamburg, after the Gestapo

had accepted your story?" I asked him.

"They made me a Hero of the Reich, and I spent three months touring the Wehrmacht camps, talking to the soldiers to boost morale."

The last night of my vigil, and seven nights after I had landed on the shores of the Sognefjord, I climbed the hill away from the mine and the prisoner compound to the edge of the Dale-Bulken-Voss road. No traffic. It was ten o'clock and the moon was bright, as it had been every night since I arrived in Norway. Cold the air was, and crisp, with the snow crunching hard beneath the skis when I could wear them, and shaking from my boots too cold to cling when the going was uphill and I unclipped the skis and carried them. I'd not yet acquired the facility for walking uphill in them.

At the pre-arranged map reference I found the stand of pines. I'd climbed the hill quickly and must have been early because I had to wait a half an hour for the ambulance. It stopped by the edge of the pines and the driver lit a cigarette. I could see his face in the light flare. I waited a few more minutes to make sure that no other vehicle was coming along the road, and then crawled forward and tapped on the door on the passenger side. He got out, went round to the back and opened the ambulance door. I darted inside, and he followed me.

"Lie on the bed," he said, "and I'll cover you up."

The warmth of the blanket was welcome. He stowed my skis and poles beneath the bed and then switched on the light. He went to a cupboard on the wall, opened it and brought out a bottle of spirits. "This will warm you," he said. I looked at him. The strain of living a double existence for two years showed in his face.

"It's a long way from Achnacarry, Klaus," I said.

"You haven't changed, Donald."

"You haven't either!"

He laughed. "Rubbish! I must look ten years older.

And my hair is grey now."

"A lot of people's hair has gone grey. Do you remember Freddie?"

"Freddie Hawkins?"

"He did a job in Italy, and when he came back, his hair had all fallen out. Came out in handfuls, over night. They had him pinned on a rock, he was balanced on one foot, and he couldn't move all night. All night long he hung on, not eight feet away from a German section. They left the following morning just before first light, and when he came down, his hair was falling out. When he got back to the rendezvous near Pisa one of his own men didn't recognise him bald, not from the back, and stuck a knife in him."

He shook his head from side to side.

"I've brought your valves," I said, bringing my hand out of the blanket. "Two 6V6's?"

"That's right."

"And I've brought you this resistor. The signals sergeant thinks a part of your transmitter's on the blink. Your transmissions are garbled in—wait a second, I have it here." I fished into my inside pocket and brought out the piece of paper. "You've got distortion over three hundred cycles, whatever that may mean. Here's the circuit diagram which'll show you which resistor it is. And will you also switch keys more often, and use your left hand more, so your sending isn't recognisable."

"You think they're on to me?"

"No, not yet. If you use the side-swipe key, and your left hand occasionally, that'll throw them."

"But they must know someone's sending from round here?"

"Keep on the move, and they'll never locate you."

He took a key ring from his pocket, inserted it into the heads of two screws, and turned. Then he put his key into the space between the rock wool slabs and pulled.

The slabs came away, revealing a flat compartment, twenty inches square and six inches deep. In it was the radio set we'd parachuted to him, an American job with three fixed frequencies. "I run a wire between a couple of trees and tap into it for an aerial," he said. "That way I never transmit twice from the same place."

"And when they take the ambulance away from you?"

"The whole lot goes into a leather case I have, marked 'X-Ray equipment, Danger Radiation'. It's been given an official inspection a couple of times by officious Gestapo guards, but nobody's ever twigged it."

"You've been lucky."

"You don't have to tell me. Have you brought any news for me. Any reports?"

He wasn't controlled through regular Army, or even S.O.E. channels. He was out on a limb, all on his own. "Be nice to him," the Brigadier had said. "Don't be your usual casual self. You can be the most off-handed devil I know. Butter him up a bit!"

"That job you did at Kristiansand," I said, "that was marvellous. With your help they were able to come straight in and get two submarines in one go. Bloody marvellous. The Brigadier said that all the credit goes to you. There's a gong in it for you, if ever you come back to England when this lot's over, a Military Cross for certain."

"I do not wish the medals," he said, though I could tell how pleased he was. We chatted for fifteen minutes, casual as if we were sitting in the lounge at the North British Hotel in Glasgow. I told him all the news I had about jobs he'd set up, heaped on the praise as lavish as marmalade. Gradually his face began to lose that drawn hunted look.

"Nobody will worry if they see the ambulance parked?" I asked him a couple of times.

The second time he grinned at me. "I've earned myself
55

a reputation," he said. "I'm afraid I've become notorious."

"In what way?"

"For picking up young girls, driving them into the countryside, and then parking the ambulance for an hour or two. They think I'm a sex-maniac."

"Bit risky?"

"Not at all. The camp commandant and I once had a foursome, right here in the back of the ambulance." We both laughed. "He brought some French champagne he'd found. They all got high on it. Dirty bastard. I didn't know at the time he liked it both ways. After he'd had the two girls, he wanted to start on me!"

"What did you do?"

"I gave him a pill. Told him it would pep him up. It put him out like a light." While I was laughing, he looked seriously at me for a moment. "What is this job?" he asked.

I stopped laughing. Suddenly. "I can't tell you yet," I said. "I really can't."

He turned away, ostensibly to get the bottle again. "I thought it might be this bigwig who's coming to visit the camp next week," he said casually. "I sent the information in one of my regular reports."

"That must have been one of the garbled ones. You'd better get that resistor in tonight. And those two 6V6's."

"He's the Area Commander of the Gestapo in South Norway. General Preise. A bastard. He ordered the Jews killed in Oslo; he started the reprisals. They say he's been responsible for at least three thousand deaths. It must be something like that—Hitler's given him the Golden Eagle personally. He was in Denmark."

"Nothing personal, is there?"

He wouldn't look at me, kept fiddling in the cupboard with that bottle. "I've got a route plan," he said over his shoulder. "I've got two, the published one and the real

56

one. I treat the local commander's piles in his own office. Last time I gave him an anaesthetic that put him out just long enough for me to look at what was on his desk. The General will be in a car a mile behind the official car. The man in there is a Feldwebel who looks enough like Preise to pass in a dim light. It's an old dodge; he's been doing it since the partisans blew his car off the road near Stavanger. They'd have killed him but the mine was faulty."

"Any reason to go for him?"

"Only psychological, I think. The partisans haven't done too well this winter. We've caught quite a number of them."

"Knock off a Gestapo officer and they have three more to take his place."

"It sounds good, that's the point. It should put new heart into the partisans."

"You've made no contact?"

"Of course not. It's too big a risk. Those two girls they took in Voss in December; the interrogating officer asked me to give them a V.D. check before he questioned them —you know the methods they use and he didn't want his staff to become infected. I think he fancied the two girls himself."

"You told him they were infected?"

"No, too risky. He might have asked for a second opinion. I injected them. With smallpox."

"Oh, my God." I'd seen the ravaging effects of smallpox on a girl's face.

"It was a risk," he said defensively, "but which do you think they'd prefer? To have their complexions ruined by smallpox, or to be raped to death by the Germans?"

"It seems drastic, that's all."

"Of course it's drastic. We're not playing games here."

"I'm sorry. I know that. Forgive me. You do what you have to. What happened to them?"

57

"They were put into isolation ward. I knew they would be, and I also knew the isolation ward isn't very well guarded. The partisans were able to get them out. Luckily the smallpox was quickly cured, and they were not disfigured."

He had sat on the opposite bunk again. "I had to take the risk, you understand," he said. "It was the only thing I *could* do. I had to get them into that isolation ward so that the partisans could break them out, and smallpox was the only way."

Now the strain lines were back again. No human being can support having to take such decisions. Not on his own, not without comfort and guidance. "I can get you out any time you want," I said, knowing what he would reply.

"I'd be useless in England taking sick parades."

I climbed off the bed. "You're a very brave man," I said, and this was not for the Brigadier. I meant it.

"Shall we go for Preise?"

"Fix your radio and check with London. If they say yes ..."

Aud Bull was waiting for me when I returned to Per Vidgren's house, at about two o'clock. She'd been sitting on my bed, and she was bent over in an uncomfortable posture where she must have slumped half asleep. She was about twenty-six or seven, tall as most Norwegians are, with long blonde hair. Though she seemed to have the bright look of healthy people who spend their lives out of doors, her skin had a texture I had seen so often, a slight greyness beneath the blood tones, the sign of too many nights spent crouched in tree bottoms, too many days burrowed away catching up on sleep. I didn't want to waken her; I felt the great compassion I experienced whenever I worked with young girls. Their bravery surpassed anything a man could know, since they ran appalling dangers of personal violation if ever they were caught. Man's a disgusting animal at the best of times, soldiers the lowest of the species, and of them all, the German soldiers were the dregs. *That* was my war, not a burning conviction that British was Best, not a quasi-political lust for nationality, not a fear of some other nation's territorial claims, but a fierce hatred of the loathesome and universal bestiality of men under arms.

Aud must have become aware that I was looking at her. Though she did not move I could tell she was awake. She'd trained herself not to move suddenly when she woke, and now she was looking at me through partly closed eyes. I turned my back and walked across to the window, giving her the privacy of wakening unobserved. The windows were heavily shuttered, of course, and sealed so no light could escape. When I turned back again she was sitting upright, her hair fingered back into tidiness, her jacket more modestly arranged.

"You're like a cat," she said, "prowling around; and we're like mice, waiting for you to pounce."

"Is it so obvious?"

She smiled, then swung her feet onto the floor.

"Don't you think we haven't asked ourselves questions," she said. "We must have the lowest success record of any unit of the resistance. Every job we do seems to go wrong. My uncle knew it, we all know it."

"Are you so inefficient?"

"We're not less efficient than any other group. Of course, a lot of what we do has to be improvised, but we do that as well as any other group."

"Then what can the reason be?"

She thought for a moment, resting her hands on the side of the bed. Sitting there, newly roused from sleep, she stirred my sexual appetites. She looked so feminine, so vulnerable. I longed to cross the room and put my arms about her. Not to protect her in sorrow, or in need, but to take her sexually, to possess her. I think she knew what I was feeling, had known it since she awoke. Perhaps, like so many women, she awoke passionate, demanding. The thought excited me beyond belief. I didn't trust myself to walk across the room and sit beside her, but I had to sit somewhere. I squatted on the edge of the table, one leg dangling. I caught a half smile on her face, as if she understood my predicament and was challenging me.

"You want me to say, is one of us a traitor?" she asked.

"I don't want you to say anything you don't feel yourself."

"You English," she said.

"I'm Scottish."

"That's even worse. You never come straight to the point. You never reveal your thoughts, never expose your-

60

selves the way a Norwegian would. I've known these people all my life. These people have all been exposed to me, and me to them. I went to school here in Loftheim with Anne and Astrid. Kari went to the same school, but she's younger and wasn't in the same class with us. Per and Tor have taken us all out at one time or another. We've all made love with Per, Tor, and Ola. Does that shock you?"

"I admire your frankness. No, it doesn't shock me."

"You wanted me to be a virgin? You'd made a mental picture of me as a virgin, a young—what do you call it—damsel in distress?"

"I hadn't thought about it." Liar. Of course I'd thought about it; one part of me was thinking about it at that very moment.

"Anne was hoping to marry Per, but he chose Kari instead. There was no resentment. Only a girl's regret."

"What about Bjornson? Have you all made love with him, too?" He was the stranger, the man from Narvik. I could understand the easy familiarity of boys and girls growing up together in what must have been a closed community. I could accept that without jealousy. But at that moment I would have hated to be told that Bjornson, too, had shared them.

"No. We haven't made love with him."

"Why not?"

She laughed gaily. "That's your Scottish nature again. You can't see the freedom we have to choose. In your mind the girls of the world divide into two kinds of people, virgins, and all the rest. You assume that a virgin will make love with nobody, except you when you marry her, but that one of the others, the non-virgins, will make love with anybody, everybody. Here in Norway we have freedom from such thoughts. Each girl chooses with whom she will make love. Either at the moment, or in advance. Do I make myself clear?"

"You do. But we're getting away from the subject of Bjornson."

Again she laughed. "Bjornson never asked us," she said.

"Why not? You're all attractive. He must have wanted you."

"Perhaps he did. Who knows? But the fact is that he never asked any of us."

"How do you know he didn't ask one of the others? How do you know he doesn't make love with one of the others?"

"Because we talk about such things. With freedom. Men and women. That's how we differ from you. That's why I cannot believe one of them is a traitor. Because to be a traitor is too large a knowledge to keep locked within yourself. Not in Scotland. Here in Norway. We'd *know* ..."

"But you don't know about Bjornson. You have never made love with him. He's not a part of your circle."

"It isn't only sex. Bjornson has been here some time. We all know him."

"And Knut?"

"Knut was born here."

"And you all *know* him?"

"Our mothers knew him better than we do."

"But you trust him?"

"He is our mayor!" She seemed surprised I should doubt him. "Knut is the one man who holds this village together. Even more than my uncle was. Knut is a man of unshakeable convictions. He would die for the people of Loftheim."

"Oh, come on now, that's a bit strong, isn't it?"

"Not too strong, believe me. When you get to know Knut as we know him, you'll realise how true it is." Now she was beginning to be angry, and I didn't want that.

"Let's go back to Bjornson. He's a fisherman from the

62

north. Why did he come here?"

"Life isn't so easy for a fisherman. Perhaps he came here for the easier life—not that we have it so very easy here either."

"But he must have had a reason for coming?"

"Life isn't like that, here in Norway. Perhaps it is in Scotland and Germany, and perhaps that's why you are fighting each other, with Norway caught in the middle. We don't feel obliged to have reasons for everything here in Norway. A man wakes up one day and doesn't like where he is or what he has become or what he is doing and walks away from all that and goes somewhere else to do something else in the hope he will become someone else."

"Bjornson is one of these men?"

"No-one has ever asked him. *You* ask him if you want to ... You know the Hardanger," she said, suddenly changing the subject, or so I thought.

"The fjord?"

"The Hardanger fiddle. It's like an ordinary fiddle, with another set of strings under the top strings. The lower set of strings cannot be plucked, but they resonate with the top strings. Some people say the Hardanger fiddle is the sound of Norway, that extra set of strings which no-one can pluck but which resonate in tune with the major chords. We're 'resonating' now in tune with the Allies. The Germans tried to make us play their tune, but they can never reach us. We're just not on their frequency."

"But meantime, you all grow older, and life withers away in your hands. The trees out there are neglected; the cattle have been taken away from the summer saeters and the winter stabburs, and young men die," I said bitterly. It all seemed such a waste of life and human purpose. Dammit, I ought not to have been talking this way with this lovely girl. I should have been holding her hand, seeing through her eyes the beauty of nature all around

63

us. She certainly sensed what I felt, and the air between us was charged, but she refused to acknowledge it. She turned her head away, and for the first time spoke without looking at me, without challenge or conviction, as if consumed by an inner doubt.

"I can't believe there's a traitor among us," she said quietly.

Now I could walk across the room. I stood beside the bed, held out my hand, and turned her face to look at me.

"You have to accept the fact, Aud."

"But I know all these people. I know them all too well."

"And I don't know them at all, is that it?"

She nodded. There were tears in her eyes.

"I'm going to find out who it is," I said gently.

She nodded again. "And then what will you do?" she asked.

"I don't know."

"May I say something? Perhaps there is a traitor. Perhaps you will unveil him for us. But, may I ask you, if you find a traitor among us, show him to us ... ?"

"Or her?"

"Or her. But then leave us to clean our own house. Don't make us more ashamed by doing our dirty work for us."

She got up and left the room. I sat on the bed smelling the fresh odour of her presence. My orders had been, 'find the traitor and kill him' as simple as that. I supposed they could be interpreted as 'find the traitor and let his own people kill him'. Or *her*, I added.

When she returned she had washed her face and combed her hair; her eyes were bright and sparkling, as if she'd been able to wash her mind clean of all doubts, all fears. Suddenly I saw her as she must have been before the start of the war. Wholly delightful, gay, desirable.

"You came here early," I said, beckoning to the bed.

64

"I was tired. I wanted to sleep a while before the meeting."

"But that's not the only reason. You could have slept anywhere."

Now she blushed prettily. "I wanted to talk with you," she said. "It seemed important to me that I should start to get to know you."

"These things happen slowly in Scotland."

"But there's so little time," she said. "Tell me, no, let me guess. You were married once. But you're not married now."

"Are you clairvoyant?" I had to explain the word to her.

"No, its not that. It's the look in your eyes. There's a sadness when you look at a woman."

"Perhaps those are my Scottish inhibitions."

Suddenly we could be gay together. And talk together about frivolous things.

"In Norway," she said, "we have an old saying. He looks heavy with love. Like when a cow is heavy with milk and can find no calf to drain her. To me you looked 'heavy with love'. Am I right? Were you married once?"

"Yes, I was married."

"I knew it. But now you are not married?"

"I'm still legally married."

"That's not what I'm talking about. The quislings think they are 'legally' in command of this country."

"In that sense, no, I'm not married."

"I would say you are a man capable of much loving. I've seen the way you look at your sergeant." Then she laughed. "Oh, what am I saying? I don't mean in that way, of course."

"Thank God for that."

"I've also seen the way you look at me. Be careful, Colonel. You are a handsome Scotsman, and we are all most lovable girls ..."

"I think you mean 'loving', don't you?"

"Loving, lovable, you know what I am talking about."

"Love can be a dangerously strong force."

"That's the Scotsman talking. Not the handsome Colonel of the British Army."

"Who badly needs a shave ..."

"There you go, afraid of the compliment. Here in Norway we are not so frightened of love as you are in Scotland; our hopes and our desires are nearer to the surface. That's another reason I cannot believe one of us is a traitor."

We both heard the footsteps, and though I knew this to be a safe house, I drew my gun and stood behind the door. Bjornson and Knut came in, shaking a fresh fall of snow from their parkas. The house was heated by a hot air system from a furnace in the cellar, as well as by wood burning stoves in each room—Per Vidgren's father had been an engineer ahead of his time—and Bjornson and Knut stripped off their outer garments.

"It'll snow all night," Bjornson said, "and that's good."

"It'll hide the tracks," Knut explained.

Kari appeared carrying a tray of cheese, herring, and the crisp flat wafer-thin bread she baked on the open fire. There was also coffee. "We get it from the German supply convoys," she said. "A man in the railway sidings at Voss is one of us."

"Dangerous ... ?"

"No; we planted it once in a soldier's camp. This coffee is meant for the officers; they think the ordinary soldiers are stealing it."

Per and Ola were late and I could see Kari was worried. They had been on an assignment, stealing ammunition for their Schmeissers and fuses and detonators too sensitive to parachute in. I was sitting in the corner of the room when Knut came and sat beside me. "You've got them all worried," he said.

66

"I know."

"Not me."

"Perhaps you have nothing to worry about?"

He chuckled. "We've heard about the English, about how you always keep your cards close to the chest."

"I'm not English."

He turned and looked at me without surprise. "I found it hard to believe you were English, speaking Riksmaal as well as you do. Few English people can manage the guttural sounds."

"It comes easily to me. I'm Scottish. We don't care for the union with the English any more than you liked union with the Danes ... or the Swedes."

"Or the Germans ... ?" he asked dryly. "Don't misunderstand me," he said. "I'm glad you've come, and I don't need to know why. We've had a run of bad luck, and we've lost confidence in ourselves. In that circumstance, it's natural to look for scapegoats, and the fear of a quisling among us is a logical one. You might help us pull ourselves together."

Easy, friendly, diplomatic. No wonder he was mayor of Loftheim, and no wonder the Germans had left him in office. But *if* he were the quisling, this would be the way to deal with me, wouldn't it? "You don't resent someone coming from outside to teach you your business? You've been running round these mountain tops all your lives."

"And where has it got us? Perhaps we may learn from you. Some of us accept that. I accept it, so does Aud. You have a valuable ally there."

"And Bjornson?"

"A simple fisherman. Used to the tides that ebb and flow. He'll come to realise what you are, who you are, why you are here, and he'll accept you. The Norwegians are very good at accepting. We have to be. Our country is so sparse, so hard, that we have to accept. Not many Norwegians run away. Even those in England just now, I

67

bet they wish they were back here. Even though life may be more easy for them. It's in a Norwegian's blood."

"Like the Hardanger fiddle?"

He bent his head forward, and then he nodded. When he lifted his head, his eyes were moist. "Forgive me," he said. "Music has been one of the strongest forces of my life. Norwegian music."

"I'd like to hear you play sometime."

He shook his head. "Come back after the war." He held out his hand. I hadn't noticed that it was misshapen. The bones had been crushed.

"The Germans?" I asked.

He smiled wryly. "That would make me a hero, wouldn't it? No, a rock fall. I could say I wouldn't have been where the rock fell if it hadn't been for the war; I could say I'd have been looked after by my friend, Doctor Ardhus, who was a specialist in bones and fractures, if the Germans hadn't killed him in 1940. But none of that would be strictly honest, would it? There'll be other bone specialists, when I can get to them, after the war."

"If they are still alive?"

"If I survive, and they survive."

Bjornson came across the room with a schnapps bottle. "I know where there will be some beer in a few days," he said. "Made in a lager, the way it used to be made. The Germans do good things if they force us to make beer in the old-fashioned way again."

I took the schnapps bottle without comment. It would take a lot of beer to fill Bjornson, I thought.

"Per's late," Knut said.

"We have no need to worry. He's a good lad. Anyway, Ola is with him, and nobody will ever take Ola by surprise!" Bjornson said. "Ola's from Bergen," he explained, "a wharf-rat from the docks. He's never done an honest day's sailing in his life. Stavanger, Bergen, Narvik, they're all the same to a wharf-rat."

68

"And you're a sailor and sailors don't like wharf-rats, wherever they come from?"

He laughed, a huge belly laugh. "You don't catch me like that, Englander," he said. "Ola and I, we know each other; there's no disagreement. Anyway, we're both too busy with the Germans to fight each other." He took the schnapps bottle from me and drank deeply. "Anyway, Englander," he said, taunting me, "why be so bloody secret about everything, looking for suspicions like a ship-board rat looks for the grain on an iron-ore boat ... yes, and finding about as much ..." He had raised his voice to encompass the whole room. "We're floundering in mid-sea, and the Englander has come over to guide us through the maelstrom. An *Englander*, if you please."

"If you must know," I said stiffly, "I'm a Scotlander."

Knut caught hold of Bjornson's parka and dragged him down on the seat beside us. "That's enough of that, Bjornson," he said, his voice breaking into the Nynorsk of his ancestors.

Bjornson was silent. No, he wasn't drunk, I guessed, and since none of the others took any notice of his out-burst I supposed they were used to hearing him speak his mind. "What's so bloody secret from us?" he said, his voice softer.

Knut said something sharp to him I didn't catch, and Bjornson was silent. Kari went out of the room and down the stairs. Aud and Anne were talking quietly with Astrid. The atmosphere was calm on top, tense below the surface. I left it as it was, to breed and to fester.

Per and Ola returned a half an hour later, Per with a flesh wound in his arm. It was nothing serious, but his hand would be stiff for a day or two. I treated him with sulphanilamide powder from my medical kit.

"Were they waiting for you again?" Bjornson asked.

"Damn bad luck," Ola said. "One man was in the woods, having a piss. He must have wanted promotion,

69

the way he came back shooting, too hurried to put his cock back in. Per got him with his first shot, but the German had nicked him."

"You get the stuff?"

"What do you think? Four boxes of ammo and four dozen stick grenades. But we didn't get any fuses."

"Damn! What good are stick grenades without fuses?"

"Take them apart and use the explosive," I suggested.

"We've more than enough explosive; it was the fuses and detonators we wanted."

"We did our damned best," Ola said, angry, but Aud placated him. "Be happy with what we've got," she said to Bjornson, then turned to me. "Bjornson always wants the impossible immediately," she said, her laugh taking away the sting. But without knowing it, she had given me the opportunity I needed.

"Then perhaps he'll be happy to know I've planned a job for tonight," I said.

There was a shocked silence. Now was the testing time. It was one thing for me to arrive dramatically from England as a saviour, quite another for them to accept me as a leader of day-to-day operations.

"We didn't know you were planning a job," Knut said, worried.

I could see they were itching to talk among themselves, but I had no intention of letting them do so. I needed to carry them all with me. "I have planned a job," I said, "and I guarantee this one will go right, if you'll do it my way, and if you'll accept me as leader. Just for this one job. Afterwards you can make up your own minds."

They were all gathered about me, but looking at each other.

"Look, this isn't the first job I've done, dammit. I could give you a list if it would impress you."

"And did all those jobs succeed?" Bjornson asked.

"Some did. Some didn't."

"And who's fault was it? The ones that failed?"

"Mine, part of the time."

"At least you don't claim to be infallible," he said.

"What's the job?" Knut asked, but I shook my head.

"I wiil not talk about the job until you've decided who is to come with me."

"How many do you need?" Aud asked.

"I could use you all."

"Then count me in." She looked around. One by one the others agreed, all except Knut.

"I need to know what the job is before I can agree," he said. But again I shook my head. "I'll tell only the people who are coming with me. Anybody who doesn't come will be left here until we get back. Here, and under guard."

"You don't trust us?" Knut said.

Now it was out. Okay, let it be said. Let them understand my reasons, my feelings, my intentions. Looking at Aud I said, "I don't trust anyone. Except myself and my sergeant."

Knut was angry, I could see that, but Aud approved. She went up to Knut. "You know he's right," she said. "Now please make up your mind to come with us. My uncle would have approved, you know that. We don't need to be *trusted*. We need to be *used*. By someone who knows what he's doing, as the colonel so obviously does. They wouldn't have sent him over here if he were an incompetent."

"All right," Knut said, "count me in for the moment. But if I think the job is impossible when I hear it, I'll say so, and do my best to talk you all out of it."

Now they all paid attention to me. "We're going to stop the generators at the mine," I said.

No-one said anything.

"We're going to stop *both* generators, the main one, and the emergency one."

71

"They'll repair them," Bjornson said, "unless you mean to destroy them completely."

"We're only going to put them out of action for a few days."

"But the engineers will fix them," Knut said.

"Ah yes, but we're going to put *them* out of action too."

"For a few days?"

I shook my head. "In their case," I said, "I'm afraid it will be permanent."

* * *

It was still before dawn when we arrived on the slopes above the mine, but there was a good moon, with frequent clouds. The diesel engine was thumping, chugging across the fjord, the smoke from the diesel curling out over the water. Four engineers lived in the building with the engine; they were used to the noise and probably would not have been able to sleep without it.

Four soldiers guarded the main gate but didn't bother to patrol the triple-strand, eight-foot-high barbed wire fence which encircled the mine in the shape of a letter U. Its ends were let into the solid rock a hundred yards on each side of the entrance to the mine tunnel. The diesel engine building was hidden from the main gate by the pre-treatment plant, which had no windows. The ends of the barbed wire fence were hidden by the same plant.

We'd go down the mountain side. On a rope. Abseil. Wearing leather mittens to prevent a burn from the rope which passes under your forearms and across your back. Some people put the rope between their legs but I don't approve that method. If you want to stop you bring your lower arm up and across your chest, and you're left hanging with the rope between your hands and round your shoulders under your armpits. The other way the rope is between your legs; I've known men be useless for

72

weeks after an emergency stop.

Per stayed at the top of the cliff with a Schmeisser ready for any Germans wandering about the minehead. Knut stayed with him. I'd originally planned for Per to come down the rope with us but I decided it was a bad idea. Not with that arm. Bjornson approved. He also approved when I went first down the rope. It was a hell of a long abseil. Bjornson came next, then Aud, then Kari. Each of us waited in turn for the next to come, holding the rope out from the rock. I felt I knew the minehead as if I'd been born there. Normally we would have scattered but back in the lee of the cliff we were out of sight. The trucks rumbled on rubber wheels out of the mine shaft and along the railway to the treatment plant without supervision. We would be spotted only if a truck came off the line. That hadn't happened while I'd been watching; the trucks were small and the bogies wide, and they were pulled along by a cogged ratchet on an endless wire rope one truck at a time. Watch the mine mouth, watch the trucks—it will be dangerous if there's a hold-up or a breakdown. The Germans are in the warmth of the mine's belly or in the treatment shed away from the wind.

When we were all down the rope we ran the short distance to the side of the diesel engine house. No-one was about. All the guards were in the guard-house, keeping warm; the engineers in the diesel house, the mine supervisors in the mine. Why not? It was snowing, and who tramps about in snow unless he's forced to? They'd all be up and about in time for the search and changeover, but I'd noticed that the minehead was quite deserted between five o'clock and half past six. Nothing ever happened here any more, and discipline is always self-relaxing. I didn't complain.

We went inside the diesel engine building, across the metal plates of the engine room, along a catwalk between the two massive machines. Only one was working, of course. The other would take its place at the changeover, eight o'clock, giving the engineers time to perform the routine tasks of daily maintenance. The engineers' room beyond the engines was closed by a solid door. I turned the handle and eased the door open. The four engineers were lying on single bed bunks, all asleep. One man was fully dressed: the engineer on duty. He'd have his ears tuned to that engine, and any change in pitch, any variation of the thump thump exhaust note would bring him immediately awake. If he were anything like other engineers I'd known, you could fire a gun next to his ear and he wouldn't hear it, but he'd always hear that engine falter. The heat in the room was stifling, and we stood perfectly still to attune ourselves to the change in temperature, to give our muscles time to recover from the numbing cold of the outside. This was the awful moment, preventing yourself from making too hasty a move, forcing yourself to stand still in the presence of those sleeping men, to acclimatise. So I played Kim's game, let my eyes quickly examine the room, memorising as many of its tableaux as I could. Last night's supper on the table, yes, but what had they eaten? Liverwurst, pumpernickel wrapped in waxed paper, butter whose surface glistened in the heat, a half-empty, or half-full, whichever way you looked at it, tin of sauerkraut. Six bottles of beer. Six. A bottle with two inches, no more, of schnapps in it. Even now, I can see that room, see the chess board on the table, with the checkmate still standing. But above all I remember the smells, of diesel, underwear, and stinking men who do not bother to wash properly.

Now the pins and needles had gone from my fingers. The men had not stirred. I flexed my muscles ready for the immediate action. Speed. Everything depended on speed.

It was easier than I had dared hope. The engineers had gone to sleep with the ventilator window closed, and had

74

banked the stove with coal which, under the draught from the chimney, had coked itself into a glowing red mass. I turned a butterfly flange and sealed off the chimney. Then, just to make certain, I lifted the centre ring from the top of the stove so the fumes of the coke would rise into the room. Pure carbon monoxide. No-one could last more than half an hour in that atmosphere, and for the last twenty-five minutes of that he'd be beyond consciousness. Bjornson gave each of them a tap behind the ear to take care of the first five minutes. Not one of them knew what hit him. We closed the door behind us. Aud and Kari were looking away from each other.

Diesel engines are water cooled. We started the second. If any one heard it, they'd think the engineers were testing it for the changeover. When both engines were running, we turned off the main water supply, took out the valve, blocked it with engineer's waste and mud, put it back in again, and turned the supply back on. No water came through our blockage. Within an hour the diesel engines would become red hot, burn themselves out, and seize. It would take a week to replace 'em.

We got out of the camp by climbing the rope hand over hand up the cliff into the snow line. On the way out I noticed our tracks leading in had already been obliterated by the soft falling snow. We stayed poised on the top of the cliff while the second line of footprints was covered by the fall. The sun broke low on the southern hills and the light of dawn touched the fjord below. The engines stopped at half past six, wisps of smoke escaping from the open windows of the engine house.

We trudged home the long way through the mountains, our eyes peeled for mobile death squads. We kept in a formation so that anyone who saw us would believe us to be Germans and avoid us. I was skiing down a long slow slope, taking it easy, not hurrying, when Bjornson came up alongside me. He lifted his goggles to permit me

75

to identify him. "Why did you want the engines stopped?" he asked.

I shook my head, and he knew better than to ask again. He dug in his poles and hastened to the head of the formation, leading the way, setting the pace.

Aud came alongside me next. I lifted my arm in greeting. She stayed beside me, taking a turn at the bottom of the slope exactly in rhythm. She made me feel like an elephant, neat though my stem turns were. After the turn she drew slightly ahead and said, "Where's your sergeant gone?"

"Oslo," I said.

She nodded. "Why did you want the engines stopped?"

I shook my head.

The way we had done the job, the Germans would believe the engineers had been accidentally asphyxiated by the monoxide fumes from the stove. Klaus could give such a verdict with a clear conscience. They would believe the engines had burned out because no engineer had been there to give them their essential hour-by-hour maintenance. We'd left the valves open, and it would take a long time to find the plug we'd put in; and when they did, they'd blame whoever had assembled the engines in the first place.

I wanted the engines stopped for a week without fear of reprisals. I wanted the Lithuanians to have a week of rest from work, to build their strength. They'd need it if they were going to survive in this climate after we'd liberated them from that hell-hole.

The following day, I slept.

When I awoke it was already dark. The road outside the house, which I could see clearly when I drew back the wooden shutters, was deserted. It had stopped snowing, and a plough had been down the centre of the road, piling the snow in banks at the sides. No-one had breached the bank in front of the house, and it was too high to step over without leaving prints. Bjornson worked for the municipality driving the plough. Knut was the mayor. So far as the Germans knew from their head count, Per, Ola, and Tor no longer existed.

Kari must have heard me moving about. She came into the attic room and stood beside me at the window. "How is Per?" I asked.

"He's going to be all right. That powder of yours seems to have stopped any infection."

"It's good stuff. I wouldn't go anywhere without it."

"Perhaps you'll leave it when you go?"

"If we haven't used it all up."

"This was a marvellous place to be, before the war," she said. "In the summer you can see the mountains from here. We knew everybody; the house was never empty, always somebody coming in to see us, and eat with us, and play music. Knut used to come and play ..."

"Before the rock fell on his hand?"

She nodded.

"How did it happen?"

"Didn't he tell you?"

"I didn't ask him."

"You're a tender person, despite all your hardness.

77

They ambushed a German boat on the Sognefjord. From the side of the fjord. There was a fall of rock. We don't know why. Perhaps the shooting set it off. A rock fell on Knut's hand. It was a stupid, pointless, one-chance-in-a-million accident ... Astrid thinks it was preordained."

"It looks that way."

"This was a happy house up until then. But that day cast a gloom on us all. Astrid's talking about 'preordination' didn't help. We have a simple belief in God; it's hard to imagine that He would be so cruel, so unnecessarily cruel."

"And the Lithuanians. Isn't that unnecessarily cruel?"

"They're in Purgatory. We believe in Heaven and Hell, you know. They're in Hell. Now Knut's in Hell; and for him it's even worse than for the Lithuanians. No-one comes to this house any more. Everyone knows we are involved against the Germans, and they don't want to compromise us."

"Or themselves?"

"No, it's not like that. They don't want to give us the burden of lying to them."

"You never had a baby?"

"I started one once. Carelessly ..."

"What happened?"

"I drank hot schnapps, and took hot baths, and went skiing furiously. An old Norwegian remedy. There's a proverb. They say you ski recklessly in the morning to take care of any recklessness of the night before ..." Her voice broke, but she didn't cry.

"When this is all over, you can be reckless again," I said.

"If I'm not too old. Or Per is not too old. Or if the Germans haven't had the use of us."

There it was again, the horrible fear that young girls have in times of war, that they will be 'used' and destroyed. I changed the subject abruptly.

78

"I want you to do something for me," I said. "Make a list of all the jobs that have gone wrong. If you can remember them, give me the names of all the people involved in each job. That's important. If you think you can't remember the name of everyone on a job, leave that job out, you understand?"

"When do you want the list?"

"As soon as possible. But, please don't tell anyone you're doing it, will you? That's very important."

"What about Per?"

"Don't even tell Per, if you don't mind."

Aud had made such a list the previous day. Knut and Bjornson were making lists now. With four separate lists to check human error, I should have good basic material.

I spent that night at the mine, alone. When I got there, I drew my parka about me and made a hide in the snow. I had a knob of cheese in my pocket, and a small bottle of schnapps. I meant to stay there for twenty-four hours.

The mine was silent. An emergency generator had been brought down from Voss, but it was not large enough to cope with the power requirements and supplied only light. The Lithuanians were in their camp, and some of them spent the day wandering aimlessly about, at a loss for something to do. Many of them stayed in their huts, except when the food truck came. I was relieved to see that Teutonic inflexibility had worked as I had hoped it would, and two meals were provided, one at seven in the morning, one at seven at night. The dowser, however, had been filled with skilly, and there was enough to go round. The Germans stayed in their barracks, except in the afternoon when the camp commandant presided at a service for the four engineers, who were shipped out of camp in the ambulance, the medical officer, Klaus, riding beside the driver. I wondered if he had guessed what part we had played in the deaths. Certainly I could detect his influence in the prisoners' double rations of skilly.

79

Late in the afternoon a truck of replacement workers arrived and they were dumped in the prisoners' compound. With no work to do, they might think they'd come to paradise. The German lorry left on time for Voss; the commandant briefly inspected the progress in stripping out the burned generators, and left in his staff car, his second-in-command beside him.

In the early evening a fight broke out in the prisoners' compound. The Germans watched but did not interfere. It was pitiful to see. Finally one of the men dropped exhausted to the ground, and the other stumbled, exhausted, away. The man lay in the snow; other prisoners walked by him, and one even fell over him, but no-one took any notice of him, lying there, freezing to death.

Late in the afternoon fresh lime was dumped over the wire into the lime-pit by enormous tipper lorries. It took three loads to cover the bodies. Shortly after dark, a light flared briefly in one of the prisoners' huts. How the devil had it been made? There were no fires in the huts, and it was inconceivable that anyone could have obtained a match. The German sentry on the gate saw the flicker at the same time I did. He levelled his rifle and fired three shots through the glassless window. I was too far away to hear any screams, and the shot caused no activity that I could see.

Shortly afterwards a train came pulling three flat-bed cars. The first car, at the front of the train, carried the usual guards and a machine-gun, the second a crane with its gantry down, and the third a generating plant and more guards. The generating plant, its wires and piping hanging beneath it had doubtless been ripped in a great hurry from the floor of some factory with a lower priority. I had to give them full marks for speed. That would teach me not to underestimate Teutonic efficiency: I hadn't expected a generator until the following day. In any case it would be four days before they could strip out the old one and install the new one; the prisoners would have at least that much rest.

I had no reason to stay after that and once it became dark I made my way back to Loftheim. I looked at Per Vidgren's white-painted house from among the trees. It was quiet and dark. I could imagine it light, echoing with happy laughter and music, perhaps the Hardanger fiddle of which Aud had spoken, played by—hadn't they said Knut would have been another Grieg if the war hadn't intervened? Or by an Ole Bull, the most famous Norwegian fiddler of them all, who had given his Hardanger melodies to Grieg. Were Aud and Ragnar Bull, I wondered, descendants of Ole Bull?

The house was too dark and too quiet. The back door was open as we had arranged it would be left if the house were safe. In that climate, no-one ever left a door open from choice. I walked slowly across the stand of trees at the back of the house, my skin prickling, my nose twitching. People have told me my nose twitches when I am worried. I was worried.

Damn me for a fool. I'd relied on the quisling's waiting until he knew what job I had come here to do. That was why I had spread the story of a big job, all-important! I had reasoned the quisling, whoever it was, would not give away the partisans or me until he'd been able to find out what that job was. It was my insurance. I thought he might have a go at Sergeant Milner, but not at me. I had thought I was safe, and with me all the other partisans who weren't quislings. No-one was in the wood behind me, I'd stake my ability as a soldier on that. You learn to listen at night, among trees. They have their own sound, and between the whisperings of branches against each other, of leaves as they pat the air, of moles and squirrels and rodents who bristle against them, there exists a silence no human can achieve. Breathing is magnified in timber at night, and the rustle of cloth and

81

leather are man-made sounds, as clearly artificial as His Master's Voice. No-one was in the timber, I was certain. But what lay ahead of me was not an empty house.

I walked slowly forward to the partly opened back door that tried to say, "Come in, everything's okay". That door led into a foyer; straight ahead the stairs went to the attic. They were black with silence. I climbed them and despite the thump of my heart, maintained an ordinary tread. I made no attempt to sneak up. Whoever was up there knew me and knew I was coming because the back window of the attic overlooked the stand of timber. I went up the stairs slowly as a tired man would, but balancing carefully on each step. I had my hand in the pocket of my parka, and in my hand I clutched a pistol. I'd get one shot only. There was not enough room in the pocket for the spent case to eject and the pistol would jam. But at least when it was in my pocket nobody would be able to knock it out of my hand or spoil my aim.

The door at the top of the stairs was closed. I opened it and walked inside. It's an old trick. As you walk forward and your left foot is swinging past your right foot, you turn your toe inwards and your left leg catches against your right leg and you stumble. It's the only way I know to do a good stumble. I did it, and missed the gun butt that doubtless would have creased the top of my head through the woollen bobble hat. As it was, the gun hit me on the base of the spine and pushed me forward, onto the carpet.

"Don't move," a voice said.

"No, Per, I won't move."

He turned on the light. I was lying on my side with my my hand still in my pocket. He was holding a Luger, but now he'd reversed his grip and the butt was in his hand, the barrel pointing at me. I lay absolutely still. A Luger doesn't kick when the trigger's pulled; it's probably the most accurate gun at short range and even though the bore is only 9 mm, it can kill just as dead as a 0.45.

"I'm going to kill you," Per said.

I looked up at him. He was at the edge of hysteria, the dangerous time when reason flees and your finger presses convulsively on the trigger, independent of your will.

"Don't talk nonsense, Per," I said quietly, humouring him the way you would a child. His cheeks were red with colour; his eyes glistened wide. But his hand was steady as a rock, and the gun didn't shake. "Put the gun away."

"I am going to kill you."

I moved my body slightly to release the hand caught beneath my body, the hand with the gun in it. Shooting that way, you can't take aim, but you rarely miss. It's almost as if your hand had an independent eye, could take its own sights. I knew I had him. I could fire whenever I wanted; he needed to pluck up his courage, and that takes time. Let him talk; that's the best way to impede action.

"*You* killed Ragnar Bull. I've worked it out. You killed Ragnar Bull and then staged that explosion to hide the traces. Now you've come here to sow suspicion among us. You tried to make us suspicious of Knut because he knew Ragnar was coming to meet you. Why shouldn't he know? He's one of us. You won't say why you've come here. Everybody says you're planning a big job, but I don't believe there *is* a job. You haven't come from England; I don't even think you are an Englander. I think you're Gestapo. Oh, very clever to pop yourself in the water a few miles down the fjord and trap Ragnar into meeting you. But then you killed him, so that you could come here and give us a hint of this big job you are planning."

Now I'd moved my hand inside my pocket; now I had a bead on him, but he couldn't see it, beneath the parka.

I didn't want to shoot him, though I was prepared to do so, if necessary. If he forced me to by making it him or me.

83

"Do you know what gave you away?" he asked, trying to taunt me. Perhaps he was worried because I wasn't pleading for my life, as he felt I should at the sight of the Luger.

"No? What?"

"These lists you're asking everybody to write. Nobody in his right mind would commit all those names and places to paper unless he were an enemy agent."

"Aud has given me her list."

"Where is it? I don't believe you."

"It's in the top drawer of that dresser."

"You're just saying that to make me look over there, so that you can put one over on me. I know it's not in that drawer. I searched all those drawers before you came back."

"Did you look *under* the drawer? That's where the list is. You don't think I'd be careless enough to leave it lying about."

No, he hadn't looked under the drawer. His eyes flicked up to the drawer, then quickly back again. "You don't pull that on me," he said.

He was standing by the open doorway. "How about this one?" I said. "Will you believe this one? Don't move, because my sergeant is standing behind you and his gun is about one inch from the back of your ear."

He smiled. "Full of tricks, aren't we?"

Sergeant Milner touched the back of Per's ear with his gunbarrel. Per hadn't heard him coming up the stairs while he was talking, but I had. I knew I must have given the sergeant a bad five minutes; I'd closed that outside door to warn him.

Per's gun drooped.

The sergeant's arm came round and grabbed the barrel, pointing it harmlessly across the room. "That's good," he said.

Per looked down at me. "I suppose this is how you caught

Ragnar Bull," he said. "I should have shot you while I had the chance."

I took the gun out of my pocket and showed it to him. "You never had that chance," I said, as I climbed to my feet. Then I backhanded him across his mouth. His top lip ran with blood. I have a hard and heavy hand.

"That's for worrying the daylights out of me," I said. "Neurotic bastards like you shouldn't be given guns to play with."

He wiped his lip with his hand. "What are you going to do, take me out and kill me?"

I backhanded him again, I was so damned angry.

Again he wiped his lip. I took his gun from the sergeant and handed it to him. Then I put my gun down, turned my back on him, and took off my parka. I hung it carefully on a hanger behind the door, then went to sit at the table.

"Put the gun away and come and sit down," I said. "Now I shall say this once to you, and then never again. I did not kill Ragnar Bull. We are not working for the Gestapo. I've come here, I've been sent here, to do a job. The Norwegian Liaison Committee in London knows all about it. I don't intend to tell you, or anyone else about it until I'm ready. In the meanwhile I want your group to help me. If you're not prepared to help me without pulling damned silly guns on me every time you think you've worked things out, then say so, and the sergeant and I will go elsewhere and make other arrangements. Hundreds of loyal Norwegians are just aching to get back in here and start messing up the Germans. I don't need you, I don't need your house, I don't need your group of partisans. So what about it?"

"It would appear I owe you an apology," he said. "I would take it as a sign that you accept my apology if you agree to stay here . . . ?"

There was a brief silence.

"You've been the victim of what is known as psycho-

85

logical warfare," I said. "You've been worked on. Somebody has made you suspicious of me, and during the last few days he's got you believing what he wants. Don't worry," I said, "I'm not going to ask you who it is. In future I'll find out things for myself and not by questioning your group. But get this fixed in your head, Per, because next time you pull a gun on me I shall kill you. *I did not kill Ragnar Bull, nor did my sergeant.*"

"I know that now," Per said.

"Right. Then remember it."

He got up to go, stuck out his hand in an embarrassed but theatrical gesture. I shook it briefly, feeling like Noël Coward. "Wipe that blood off your face before Kari sees it," I said, "or she'll be after me with the rolling pin."

"The rolling pin?"

"Never mind ..."

*   *   *

Sergeant Milner had grown a luxurious beard.

"The barber for you, my lad," I said.

He smiled ruefully. I think he'd fancied himself a Don Juan.

"Don't worry, it's my turn next."

He stuck his head over the table, and I put a handkerchief beneath his chin. With scissors borrowed from Kari I cropped his beard close to his face and his hair close to his head, keeping the trimmings in a neat pile on the handkerchief.

We changed positions and he did the same for me. My beard was soft, silky, and damned hard to cut. Thank God there was no mirror in the room.

"Couple of days to grow again," I said, "another trim, and we'll pass." I put the woollen cap back on my head and gave him his hat. "Put it on and keep it on, though you'll need to take it off outside." The woollen hat prickled

86

my scalp and I wanted to scratch, but didn't.

"It's very cold out there, sir," he said.

"I know. Better get used to it."

He looked at me. I looked at him.

"What were you going to say, sergeant?"

"Mind you wrap up well, sir...."

*   *   *

Ragnar's radio was buried underground in the timber at the back of Per Vidgren's house, in a leather case with a waterproof lining. We swept off the pine-needle carpet, lifted the timber lid, and brought out the radio, the battery, the key and headset equipment. As soon as we were outside the stand of timber we took off our bobble hats. I had left my parka in the radio hole, and now wore a woollen overcoat that had belonged to Per Vidgren's father and was only thick enough for the spring. The sergeant was similarly dressed. We were both bloody cold. We raced up the side of the hill as fast as we could go to keep the blood flowing in our veins. I had lost all feeling in my unprotected ears by the time we got to the ledge below the summit. We drove the two aerial spikes into the compacted snow on a compass bearing, and stretched the aerial between them. I plugged the aerial into the socket, my gloveless fingers sticking to the metal. When I switched on, the needle climbed rapidly. "Plenty of juice in the batteries, give them credit for that," I said. It took only three minutes for the set to heat up and for me to freeze, sitting huddled inside that inadequate overcoat. The sergeant's face looked blue in the moonlight. "Rub your ears with snow," I suggested.

"I would, if I thought I could find them, sir," he said.

I sent the call signal, then switched to receive and waited. No reply. With a fixed frequency set you can't spin a dial, listening for your call sign. You sit there, tapping a key and waiting, wondering if your valves are right, if they're working, or if, a fraction to the left or right of your frequency, the other station is batting out an urgent signal. I tapped the key again. "Able Fox Able, to Baker Baker Baker, Report my signals, over." This time he came in immediately and nearly blew the phones off my ears. Or was that the effect of the cold? I turned down the volume, then started on my prepared message, sending thirties fast and clean. I knew he'd read them at that speed. He sent me a Roger and Out, and I switched off. Duration of transmission, forty-five seconds. Speed down the mountainside, approximately forty-five miles an hour, me with a battery on my back and skis parallel, crouched to cut wind resistance. I'd even wax lacquered the underside of the runners. We saw no one. Down by the tip of the fjord, across from the mine and the prisoners' camp, we hid in a patch of timber. I spread a blanket of pine needles an inch thick, to keep me off the ground, and we sat beneath the trees, listening to the thud of the small diesel engine.

"How did your trip go?" I asked.

"Very well, sir."

"Thank God you came back when you did."

"That closed door gave me a shock."

"It was meant to. You got on all right?"

"Yes, sir."

"You don't want to tell me about it?"

"Not particularly. It got a bit messy."

"But it went all right?"

"Yes, sir."

Usually an informer works to only one contact, the way a copper's nark gets his drinks from one copper only. We had reasons to believe one man in the Gestapo headquarters was receiving more than his share of information about the activities of the partisans. And the devil was being selective about which information he used.

Some jobs he let go through, others he stopped. Sometimes he let the partisans get away with it, at others he put the whole lot in the bag. It was happening throughout southern Norway. Occasionally, despite the Gestapo's vigilance, prisoners did escape, and one name cropped up again and again—Major Hans Boghral. All the escapees, at one time or another, had been questioned by Major Boghral. At first we had thought Boghral was the ace interrogator, but then we'd had reports that he had been active in the field, and interrogators didn't usually move out of headquarters. We'd put Boghral under surveillance, a difficult job involving three Norwegians dropped in especially from England. One by one they'd been picked up. It became apparent that Boghral had infiltrated the partisan groups; perhaps he'd perverted people already in the partisans, by what method we couldn't tell.

Many a man would rather betray his country than reveal his own weaknesses. Informers in war time were men who, in peace time, had been, or would be, embezzlers, homosexuals, pimps, rapists, or even power-hungry, position-seeking despots. The strength of the Norwegian partisans was that Norway didn't have a large criminal element in the population, didn't have many of those dregs of humanity from which the Gestapo could draw its recruits.

Boghral had a weakness, however; he kept a male 'friend' in a house outside Voss. Our third Norwegian had uncovered and reported that situation before Boghral caught him.

Sergeant Milner's assignment had been to get into that house and kill Boghral. "It got a bit messy," he'd said. No doubt he'd had to kill the 'friend' too.

I put my arm beneath my head and lay down. On the other side of the tree the sergeant did the same. I lay there staring out over the fjord, listening to the chug of that engine, watching the smoke trails float gently over the water. It was late and the moon was low. The mine was a blaze of light and I could see the small figures of construction engineers bustling about, preparing the parts of the new engine before moving it into the engine house. The charnel house. Six men dead already, seven if you included Boghral's 'friend'. Once I swore I'd never kill a man. I thought I'd never need to; disable him temporarily perhaps, but never kill him. There's never any need for man to destroy man, I told myself. Seven dead, and if Per's finger had tightened on that gun, another would have died. Him or me.

I was cold.

I turned over and cradled the other ear in the shoulder of that nearly useless coat. Thank God it wasn't actually freezing; the last thing I wanted was to return to England with frostbitten ears. Do you lose your hearing, I wondered, with frostbite? I'd never thought to ask the survival medico.

I didn't know it, but I was rubbing my ears.

"Don't rub them, sir," Sergeant Milner said. "You'll only make them worse!"

I closed my eyes. The thump of the diesel seemed to die down when I wasn't looking across the fjord. I thought about warm things, fur-lined parkas, anoraks, black boots with sheepskin lining. I thought of hot soup, bacon on toast, oat cakes fresh from the oven. But above all I thought of bed and Betty's arms around me. Slowly, insidiously, the thump of that diesel increased again until it seemed to be inside my head, drowning out my warm thoughts. Only a few hours remained until dawn, but it was going to be a long cold night, nevertheless. "Never mind," I said to the sergeant to cheer myself up, "General Preise tomorrow!"

Aud commented on our dress when we arrived at the rendezvous with the partisans.

"What's happened to your parkas?" she asked. "You'll freeze to death in those overcoats."

"We're testing thermostatic underwear."

"From the way you're shivering, it's useless!"

"They tried thermostatic underwear in northern Norway before the war," Knut said, taking me seriously. "It wasn't much good. It didn't breathe the way wool does."

Bjornson was looking at us as if we were crazy. I felt he'd made a pact with himself not to be surprised at anything we did. But he put his hand on my shoulder, then patted the centre of my back between my shoulder blades. He knew I wasn't wearing anything special beneath that cold old tweed. But he made no comment, and I didn't volunteer any information.

The secondary road from Bergen to Voss runs through mountainous country and snakes round the edges of a couple of fjords. For most of the way it has been cut into the mountain side, but at one fjord the rock is so steep a road bed could not be hacked into it. Norwegian road engineers are accustomed to that problem; their solution is to put the road on a shelf which hangs along the side of the mountain. Above the shelf they build a pitched roof to throw the snow and any rock falls over the road into the fjord below. Travelling a road like that is an awesome experience for a nervous person; the fjord lies below and the mountain stands above, and only the brackets of the shelf prevent the roadway from tumbling into the water.

The brackets are made of baulks of timber twelve inches thick and their ends are secured into the rock itself on metal plates. The baulks are slotted to fit together into an intricate pattern like the roof timbers of a house turned upside down; they are held together by bolts two inches thick, screwed and nutted at each end.

It was a simple matter to take off the nuts and prise the bolts back through the timbers with a crowbar. Bjornson had practical training; he and Sergeant Milner worked out the details between them while I watched.

Knut had brought a set of bolts similar to the ones in the road, but his were sheared in the centre. They inserted the sheared bolts in two halves, one on each side of the hole. It looked as if the bolts were still in position, and they could pass any inspection, but we knew they wouldn't hold.

Bjornson and the sergeant were working out stresses and loads. "We've got a problem, sir," the sergeant said. He and I both had a problem: how to keep warm. He was better off than I was. At least he was working, while I was standing around watching, frozen to the marrow.

"What's the problem?" I asked.

"We can't be very accurate about the weight of the timbers, sir. They're soaked by water and ice. If we take out too many pins the road will drop under its own weight without a car on it. If we take out too few it don't drop at all, not even with a car on it. It's a handicap not knowing the weight of the car."

The sergeant and I were the only ones who knew at this stage that General Preise would be in the second car, a mile behind the first. The bridge had to hold when the first car went over, then collapse under the weight of the second. We did have one thing in our favour: the general's car would be much heavier. Completely protected by half-inch armour plate, it weighed as much as a small tank. But the road must not collapse either before or after the first

92

car. We were praying a loaded lorry wouldn't arrive at that precise moment, but lorries didn't use this road—that was a reason the general would be on it.

"Why don't we just blow the road?" Ola asked. "The simple approach. You people make everything so complicated."

"I'm trying to avoid reprisals," I said without anger.

"Damn the reprisals. If we all felt like that, we'd never do anything," he said.

What had Bjornson called him? A 'wharf-rat'? His philosophy was to get in quick, get out quick, grab what you could and damn the consequences. Ten to one if he did this job, the road would break too soon. But would that be because of his own impatience, or because he was warning General Preise? Was Ola the man I was looking for?

"Whatever happens, this road mustn't collapse before the general gets here," I said.

"It's safe to take out three more pins," Bjornson insisted.

Would three pins drop the road? Was Bjornson the man anxious to give the game away to General Preise?

"Take out three more pins," Bjornson said, shaking his head at the sergeant's obstinacy. "Look, trust me, I know about these matters."

Anne, Kari and Astrid were on watch at each end of the overhang. We were among the timber beneath the shelf, well out of sight of anyone who came along. Per and Tor were each half-way between us and the girls. Ola, Aud, Knut, Bjornson, and the sergeant were doing the work. I was watching. And freezing. Suddenly Per gave a long low whistle. We crouched back under the shelf, only a few feet above the fjord.

Something was coming along the road.

"Move away from here," I insisted, "just in case you miscalculated...."

We scuttled away from the sabotaged baulks. Now we could hear the engine of the vehicle on the road. "Don't let it be a tank," I prayed. I couldn't see what it was, but it didn't rumble like a tank. It got to the end of the wooden shelf and I held my breath for a moment. It was being driven slowly. Klaus had said nothing about this, but I guessed it was an advance car sent to inspect the roadway. The car slowly traversed the shelf. As it drew near the sabotaged portion, the timber baulks began to creak ominously.

Bjornson must have seen the expression in my eyes. "There's always a bit of a creak," he said, smiling, confident. The vehicle came slowly on, and again we heard that ominous creak; and then I saw one baulk of wood press against another and, liberated by the split pin, push a wedge of timber as big as a piece of cheese off the joint. The baulk moved about six inches. All the baulks seemed to be moving, and to my over-fertile imagination the whole roadway seemed to sag, but Bjornson was smiling and I looked along the baulks and saw them ripple upwards as the vehicle passed over them onto the safe roadway beyond. Once it had arrived at the edge of the shelf, we sighed in relief. "What did I tell you?" Bjornson said. "We could take out at least five more pins."

"Make it three," I said.

"But that won't be enough."

"I tell you make it three," I said and scrambled back. For a moment I thought he would rebel.

Knut was looking at me. "What are you expecting, a tank? It would take a tank's weight to crack the bridge if they could drive that vehicle over safely."

"We're waiting for a loaded lorry," I lied.

He nodded his head. "Ah, I understand now," he said, and he turned to Aud, Bjornson and Ola. "We're waiting for a loaded lorry," he said.

"What's in it?" Aud asked.

"I don't know. Better ask the colonel. He gives out information like a Danish sea captain."

Aud turned to me, but she knew I'd have nothing to add.

"Come on," Bjornson said. "If we're going to get out three more pins, we'll have to hurry."

They took out three more pins while I watched more carefully than ever. The shelf didn't seem to shift while they were doing it. Then we retired almost to the ends and waited. I was at one end of the shelf with Aud, Per and Knut. The sergeant was at the other with everyone else.

"They're due at midday?" Aud asked.

"Yes. Within five or ten minutes."

"If they started on time," Knut said, "from wherever they—whoever they are—are coming."

They were on time. To the minute. I heard Kari's whistle at twelve o'clock exactly. Then heard the sound of an engine. The vehicle was doing about thirty miles an hour; I heard him change down when he came to the end of the shelf, then drive over at about twenty-five. Everyone was tense, watching the section we'd sabotaged. I held my breath, but for a different reason. Had I miscalculated when I'd said take out three more pins? I didn't think so. Sergeant Milner would have found some way to correct me unobtrusively if I had been wrong. The car arrived at the edge of the sabotaged section. The road sagged, but by now I was used to that. The road appeared to sag whatever was on it, but the cantilever of the baulks was so arranged that what appeared to be considerable movement down here would be insignificant on the roadway itself. They'd have to allow for expansion in hot weather, contraction in the winter. The car was in the centre of our section. I looked at Knut. His face was worried.

"I don't think it's going to go," he said, "I don't think it's going to fall."

I prayed it wasn't.

The car ran over the remaining section and off the shelf, leaving the woodwork intact. Knut turned to me.

"All that work for nothing! Bjornson said we could take out *five* pins."

I knew the sergeant would be subjected to the same barrage of objections. "Stay exactly where you are," I said.

"We might as well go," Aud said. She started to move along the baulk.

"Stay where you are, Aud," I said. "I mean it."

She stopped absolutely still. Was I giving her an *order*? I could see her look at Knut and Per.

Thirty miles an hour is one mile every two minutes. Could I hold them two minutes without producing a gun? Once I put a gun on them, there'd be no going back.

The sergeant had run along the baulks and was working with a crowbar in the centre of the sabotaged section. He'd have done the same sums I had. A mile in two minutes. He had less than a minute to get back to safety. Assuming the car behind, the one in which the general was actually riding, had maintained its distance. I was watching the sweeping second hand of my watch.

"I don't see any point in staying," Knut said, but without vehemence. "Anyway, what's the sergeant doing?"

Aud was smiling. "That wasn't the vehicle you were after," she said.

I smiled back at her. "You deserve a coconut for that," I said.

"A coconut?"

"Forget it. It's an English expression."

Kari and Astrid were watching the road from the roof of the snow-shed. Suddenly I heard one of them whistle. I glanced back at the sergeant. He was scuttling along the baulks, back to his previous waiting position.

The car was approaching. I could tell immediately by the squeak of the shelf and its initial sag that this vehicle was much heavier. This would be the Mercedes, with the armoured plating that brought the car up to six and a half tons deadweight. The shelf squeaked and groaned, the baulks moved and I had to reassure myself their movement wouldn't be apparent on the roadway itself. Think again of the cantilever principle, I told myself; one inch of movement up there means a foot of movement down here. There was still time for the car to stop. I had heard no gear change but a Mercedes might have a preselector gearbox which shifted gears automatically and smoothly. Now the vehicle was approaching the centre section; now it was on it.

The baulk of timber at the edge of the section moved downwards twelve inches, shearing off the shoulder of timber it had been bolted to; the bolt, severed in the middle, gave it no support. Another baulk moved down with a hideous groaning sound, and then a baulk started to cantilever outwards under the pressure.

"It's going," Knut said.

It was the first time I had seen him excited. It *was* going. The collapse took place relatively slowly and the driver must have realised what was happening. He put his foot on the accelerator, but the surge of power in the back wheels no doubt abetted the destruction. Suddenly the roadway collapsed with the car on it. I caught a quick glimpse of a black-and-green Mercedes saloon, and the arm of a man in uniform sticking out of the back window, and then heard the whole downwards rumble of car and baulks and roadway and rocks, and the revving of the engine now that the wheels were disengaged, and the shouts of the car's occupants—or was that my fancy?— and the ear-splitting crash as the debris hit the fjord.

There were no survivors. We waited five minutes in case the car had taken a bubble of air down with it, but the fjord was still and dark and deep, and though the timber baulks floated to the surface, of the Mercedes and its occupants no single trace remained.

I looked hastily at one of the sheared bolts. It appeared to have a natural break. With half the bolt left in the timber, no one would suspect sabotage. What was the reprisal price of a Gestapo general? A Gestapo Feldwebel had been ambushed and the Germans had taken fifty lives; God knows how many they would have wanted for a general!

We climbed the hillside overlooking the fjord, then sped away on skis. Despite the wind that pierced the overcoat, I was warmed by success, exhilaration, and movement. One Gestapo general less may not matter in the long run. Another would take his place as soon as he was found dead, some Gestapo colonel who'd been sitting on his knife waiting for promotion. But the deaths of the Jews in Oslo, the partisans who'd refused—in Aud's and Bjornson's phrase—to bend the knee, they at least had been revenged. And that thought was heart-warming, even if it did nothing for my frozen body.

Later that night, the sergeant and I shaved a stripe down the centre of each other's head from brow to nape, and splashed each other with gentian violet solution.

"Why don't you ever smile?" people always said to me. I'd reply, "My face is solemn in repose," and they'd say, "Miserable bastard," or if they didn't say it, I knew they were thinking it. I had always been tall and gaunt. No matter how much I ate, I never put any weight on. I was strong enough all my life, but thin, painfully thin to hear my mother talk. I cannot remember a time when my mother wasn't looking at me with anxious eyes and urging me to have another spoonful of something or other. "Go on, Donald, get it down. It'll put some flesh on your bones."

But it didn't, and her face remained wistful and pleading and anxious right up to the day of her death in 1939. She'd had me late in life and never forgave herself; wrongly she supposed that by carrying me at an 'advanced' age she had denied me the full complement of flesh on my bones. She died blaming herself, as neatly and with as little trouble as she had always lived, of a blood clot that killed her within an hour.

I was of an age to tell myself I could get along without her. The war came and I put her to the back of my mind and joined up immediately. I thought about her when my marriage to Betty went wrong—I knew she would have given me some careful but forthright advice, against which I would have rebelled, and somewhere in the middle I would have known what to do. I missed her, perhaps not so strangely, when my body was cold, hunched in that inadequate overcoat.

I'd been wearing a British Army warm when the Brigadier called me into his office in Ebury Street. He had a

99

fire going in the grate and he was standing there, warming his backside. I took off my overcoat, and he moved along to make room for me. "Nippy outside, Captain," he said. It felt wrong, standing at a blazing fire next to the Brigadier, warming my arse, but it was his way of putting me at my ease. When we sat down at his desk, the seat of my pants scorched me behind the legs.

"This is a rotten job," he said, looking as if he regretted sending me.

I nodded. It was always a rotten job. They never realised, when they formed Special Services, how many rotten jobs there would be. It was all supposed to be black faces, and woollen helmets pulled down tight, and crawling across the beaches. It was all supposed to be derring-do and 'Up the Team', with brilliant men to lead you through the dangers of war-time Europe as if you were at play.

But gradually the jobs got to be more rotten. Very often the only way to bring a situation to an end was to kill somebody in circumstances that made it murder, no matter which convention you were playing. The Special Operations Executive had been formed to drop people back into their own homelands, to work radio networks and to feed back information about troop movements and the locations of ammunition trains and dumps. But all too often they became counterspies, very often they also became judge and executioner. When the names were known in advance, someone in a War Office dungeon called in Special Services rather than waste valuable nationals. And Brigadier Clyde Rogers, V.C., M.C. and bar, was the man who gave out the jobs. If he hadn't lost an arm and an eye at Dunkirk, he would have preferred to go himself rather than to sit at the wrong side of that desk saying, "It's a rotten job."

"It's really two jobs in one," he said. "There's been some talk of launching our second front in several places simultaneously, and one of the sites chosen is in Norway.

Near a place called Voss. We could get a lot of men in there and use it as a base to strike down into Denmark and Germany, but, more important, we could use it to take possession of the Skagerrak and the Kattegat and the North Sea approaches. And we could close the Baltic. Now let me be quite specific. This is a hare-brained plan, one of several the Strategic Committee has come up with. I personally don't think it has any chance of success, and I know for certain that Mountbatten is against it, Monty's against it, and Winston himself will never give it his support. But meanwhile we have to go through the motions. Discreetly."

"What about the local boys in Norway?"

"That's the rub. They've been infiltrated. One of them has gone wrong, but we don't know which one."

"S.O.E.?"

"They don't want it. It's a killing job. We know the contact, a Gestapo officer called Boghral, and he has to be killed for a start to make the quisling find new contacts. And then the quisling has to be stopped."

"And there are problems?"

"Yes. It's a small community. Everybody knows everybody, everybody vouches for everybody. Anybody who goes in there and knocks one of them off will have to make it absolutely convincing."

"You said there were two jobs?"

"The other one's quite conventional. Titanium. Strategic War Supplies. It's mined in Norway, the Germans' only supply. We've knocked out the mines at Kirkenes; we're ready to blast the few mines that are still operating along the coast whenever we like. But there's one mine, near Voss, slap in the middle of our area, and it supplies more ilmenite—that's titanium ore—than all the rest put together. Now, if we knock out all the other mines, that mine near Voss will suddenly have an enormous strategic importance for the Germans, and they'll move in more troops to guard it even more closely than they do at the moment. And it's right in the middle of the area we'll be interested in, if this second-front plan is ever adopted."

"Knock out the mine permanently, and they'll withdraw the guards, eh?"

"That's the theory."

"And how do we knock it out?"

"That's where the rotten part comes in. We've seen plans of the mine drawn up by a man called Vidgren. We've also seen a report he made to the Norwegian Ministry of Mines. That mine's a death-trap. The Germans know it, and they're using Lithuanian forced labour. The mine isn't properly ventilated."

"So, one spark?"

"You've got it. They take precautions, of course. All the trolleys have rubber-coated wheels; all the lights are mounted in sealed units behind armoured glass; and, of course, the Germans take damned good care the Lithuanians have no matches or any other means of starting a fire. But it's still a death-trap. Seems there's a thrust fault in there, and the ore is mixed with gases from decaying vegetation. Marsh gas."

"And the Lithuanians are breathing it."

"They die. Twenty a month. It's a living death."

"The bastards. The Germans could give them respirators to work in."

"They did, apparently, at first. But it cut output by thirty per cent. They'd rather lose the men than the ore. Men can be replaced."

He was silent, sorry he'd said that. If the job failed the men he sent in would have to be replaced.

"It's a rotten job," he said. "And there's only one way to do it. From inside the mine. We've had a planning section on it. Someone could do it and get out again, if he was nimble. But it'd be touch and go."

"How'd the boffins suggest it be done?"

102

"They've worked out an ingenious scheme. It's a wafer, thin as paper. It has a backing. You take two wafers, peel the backing off them, stick them together, and fifteen minutes later they start to splutter and spark. It would mean being in the mine at the end of the shift, planting the wafer, leaving the mine with that shift. The mine would blow before the next shift went in. It'd bring down the mountain. The Germans would never get it working again in time."

"A one-man job?"

"The old Army principle of one equals two. Take another man in to cope with the Gestapo man, Boghral. And to get out and confirm a recommendation for a bit of ribbon!"

"What about the quisling?"

"He'd show himself, or so the planning committee think."

The Brigadier got up and stood by the fire. "Like some tea?" he asked, and turned the old-fashioned porcelain handle that would ring a bell in some servant's quarters somewhere. It was that kind of a house, taken over for the purposes of war.

The tea came. On a tray. In Minton cups. He lifted the top of a biscuit barrel. "Dammit," he grumbled, "you'd think they'd give us digestive biscuits."

"Rank should have *some* privileges."

"Yes, and by the way, if you do this job, we'll be making you up to Lieutenant-Colonel."

"A bribe?"

"No. So that you can show a bit of rank to the partisans. Make them feel important."

I munched one of the plain tea biscuits, sipped from the cup. "You've decided I'm the man for it, Brigadier?"

He nodded.

"On what basis, may I ask?"

He didn't reply immediately. He finished his tea, put

103

it back on the tray, went and sat behind his desk. Then he looked at me. Country-house upbringing, Eton, Sandhurst, the Guards of course, nothing in his background prepared him for this moment. A private Educational Establishment in Aberdeen, Dollar Academy, Edinburgh University and the Royal Artillery, nothing prepared me for it either. He looked at the fingernails on his one remaining hand. He lifted his monocle and put it into his one remaining eye, using it to read the papers on his desk. Then he opened the lids of his eye and the monocle dropped to hang on the thin red line from which, in every sense of the expression, it was suspended. "You've done this sort of thing before with success; you speak the local lingo; you're not doing anything else at the moment; and like the rest of us you're quite expendable."

"But why specifically *me*? A dozen men have those qualifications."

He had the grace, or was it the sense, to smile. "You have one unique qualification," he said. "The boffins of the planning committee think that it would be impossible to get into the mine passing as a German. They all know each other too well. Also, the chances are that if a German went into the mine alone, the Lithuanians would eat him alive. That's how hungry they are, and how desperate."

Suddenly the words of my mother came back to me. "Have another spoonful, Donald. Put some flesh on your bones!"

"Whoever goes in there," the Brigadier continued, "has to pass himself off as a starved-to-death Lithuanian. If you don't mind my saying so, you have just the face for it."

The train was late. I lay up against the fence, half-way along the shunt line. No lights; not even the shaded lamps I could see on the platforms of Voss station. One goods train had come through, but hadn't stopped. Soldiers around the station, but none guarded the shunt line. One soldier patrolled the UP line, a rifle slung on his back and friends joking at his bad luck. Two walked the DOWN platform, luckily without a dog. The station itself was crowded with all ranks going east to Oslo, west to Bergen. The Granvin loop line evening train came in early and stood mournfully sighing, with two coaches behind the locomotive, a flat car on the back carrying what looked like a piece of field artillery beneath a tarpaulin.

There were no civilians in sight, and the waiting room and the refreshment room were closed and dark. The railway transport officer's hut beside the station entrance was buzzing with soldiers; a plume of smoke rose from its chimney, but lost itself in the night sky. The moon had not yet risen, but I knew it couldn't be long delayed. There'd been a lot of cumulus about during the afternoon, and no winds to shift it. The winds would come later, about ten o'clock, and then the countryside would be bright as daylight. One of the shackles Klaus had supplied was fastened round my left wrist. I'd worn it for two days on each wrist in turn, treating the burns it caused with the sulphanilamide powder into which I'd mixed powdered wood charcoal. The wounds were open and black but free from infection. I held that hand in my overcoat pocket to minimise the chink of the wrist shackle on the chain of the coupling. In my left hand I held the long steel needle that fitted into the piping of the overcoat which Klaus had also supplied, along with the trousers, the shirt, and the boots. I was wearing thermostatic underwear, and contrary to what Knut had said, it did help. Sergeant Milner was lying in the fence bottom behind me. "You all right, sir?" he whispered.

"Yes," I said, then added, "Thank you."

"Train's late."

"It'll be here, if Aud was right."

She was right, of course. I heard the train chugging up the slope to Voss. It was a long train with goods carriages, a platform at the front carrying guards and a machine-gun, several flat cars of heavy artillery no doubt destined for the Bergen defence system. Tacked on to the end, behind the guard's truck, was a high-sided, open, cattle truck. The engine went past the station and stopped. We heard the clank of points, saw a soldier uncouple the last car. We heard the whistle and the train started back. When that last carriage, the cattle truck, had passed the points the train braked, but the cattle truck carried on down the shunt line under its own momentum. The train went quickly forward, wheels sparking on the lines.

No-one appeared to notice the cattle truck trundling slowly in the dark like a ghost train. There was a bend in the shunt line and the sergeant and I ran forward out of sight of the train and the station.

I grabbed the metal ladder that ran up the side of the cattle truck and almost cried out with pain, it was so cold. I pulled myself into the air, and fumbled with my feet on the bottom rung. The sergeant leaped on after me. I heard him hiss as his hands touched the frozen metal. At the top of the ladder I swung myself along the side of the truck, compressing my silhouette as low as possible, sliding along the plate to make room for Sergeant Milner. We could see nothing in the cesspool below us, but the smell was almost overpowering. The truck continued slowly along the shunt line, its velocity neatly gauged by the engine driver; finally it reached the end of the line and collided with the steelplate bumper set in a block of concrete. At the instant of collision, we dropped down inside. I landed on a shoulder, and the victim went down with a grunt. It was just one more blow in a journey full of blows. These were the oxen of the labour force, those most able to work, those who'd given the Germans no reason to annihilate them. Their spirits were crushed, though not, I hoped, beyond repair. I felt no-one draw away from me, no-one draw near to me. They stood like cattle in water, absolutely immobile. I took a shackle out of my pocket, unwound its short coupling then reached forward and found the chain that ran from front to back of the cattle truck. When I had found it, I passed the shackle behind it, and wriggled my left hand into it. It was a tight squeeze; it had to be to remain convincing. The sergeant coughed in the arranged signal; I knew he too was safely shackled to the chain. I could hardly breathe for the stench. The bottom of the truck had been spread with what felt like straw; at one time it must have been clean. No-one spoke. I heard the sound of someone urinating against the side of the truck, and later smelled a defecation close by.

About an hour later a lorry approached, and I heard the grind of the low reverse gear as it backed up to the truck. Almost at the same time the moon came out, and for the first time I could make out the people nearby. Between the sergeant and me were two individuals with heads cropped as ours were. One had a stubbled chin; since the one nearest the sergeant had a smooth chin I guessed she was a woman. Her arms were held loosely in front, as were all our arms, hanging from the shackles round the chain. Beyond the sergeant a man, distinguishable again by the stubbled chin, was hanging on the chain itself. He seemed to be dead. I turned round and looked the other way along the truck. The man behind was standing close to me but not leaning on me. His mouth was partly open and his teeth were brown stumps in his gums. His eyes were fixed in my direction, but utterly devoid of expression. He seemed to be looking a million miles beyond me and, incredible though it may seem, he was smiling. But it was the vacant smile of an idiot.

Twenty prisoners stood in the truck. How long they'd been there I couldn't tell. When the side door slammed down, they made no sign. I heard a German voice in the doorway. "Um Gottes Will, this is a bad one ..." he said. I felt the chain moving along its length, turned and shuffled forward with the others.

The lorry had been placed so that we walked along the dropped door of the truck straight into the lorry. I could see a German ahead, dragging the chain. In comparison to the emaciated prisoners, he looked monstrously huge, with a fat beer belly on him. He took the chain to the front of the lorry and passed it through, and another soldier locked it on the other side of the hole. As he came back down the lorry, he reached with his stick and the first prisoner lifted his left arm to reveal the inside of his wrist. The soldier came all along the line, looking at wrists. When he got past the sergeant, the man who had been slumped on the chain was half lying again. The soldier put his stick under the man's head and lifted it.

"Another dead one," he called, and let the man's head sag again. We were driven to the titanium mine with the corpse among us. Once or twice I glanced at the sergeant. He had one hand on the chain, and the other braced against the side of the truck. He looked at me, raised his eyebrows slightly, then threw his eyes out of focus, the way we'd practised staring at a stick three feet away, then looking through and beyond it. It helps if you squint slightly. I wanted him to move his hand from the side of the truck but then saw the laceration where the motion had flung him against the side. His cheek was bleeding through the oil and charcoal and sulphanilamide powder we had rubbed in to give us at least some protection against infection.

The journey to the mine seemed longer than our marathon up the Sognefjord. When we arrived the driver, sadistic bastard, braked and then reversed quickly, catching us all by surprise. We collapsed into a heap at the bottom of the truck, as far as the chain would permit us to fall. We heard the barbed-wire gates dragged aside, then the tailboard dropped and the first man was prodded out with sticks. The man in front of the dead man had to drag him out; the sergeant helped and they threw the corpse onto the ground. The rest of us had to jump off the truck past it, sliding our shackles off the chain. Just outside the compound was a blacksmith's anvil. As each of us came from the truck he was prodded forward to the anvil to lay his wrists and shackles across its flat face. The blacksmith used a cold chisel and a hammer and with one blow cut through the riveting pin so the shackles could be unhinged. We dropped our shackles into a waiting wooden box. The officer at the gate again checked that we had a number on our wrists, but he made no note of it. When the man in front of me stepped to the anvil, the blacksmith swung his hammer wide and hit the chisel a glancing blow. The chisel head banged into the prisoner's wrist, and he screamed with pain, but the blacksmith took no notice. He put the chisel back into position and swung the hammer. A residual spark of fear remained in the prisoner's eyes, he flinched in-

109

voluntarily and the chisel came away from the pin and the hammer hit the anvil. Now he's for it, I thought, eyeing the blacksmith and the hammer he wielded so clumsily. But the officer jabbed the prisoner into the compound, the shackles hanging from his bloodied wrist. Poor bastard'll have to live and work with that on, I thought, and held each of my wrists steady when the moment came for the blacksmith to free me.

I longed to rub my sore, chafed wrists, but none of the other prisoners did, so despite the temptation, I left them alone. The last pins severed, the last shackles removed, the blacksmith swung his anvil effortlessly onto the back of his pick-up, the officer got into his staff car, the four sentries dragged the barbed-wire gates across the compound entrance, and we were left in the prisoner compound, so far as anyone knew two more just like the others. Men without names, with numbers on our wrists that didn't mean a thing, men who'd been condemned to die a cold, lonely, miserable death when the last erg of our work energy had been extracted from us.

Not one man but a nation did this, not one man but a system, a belief, a way of life, a style and code of conduct. Every single person, soldier or officer, on the long shameful route obeyed his orders. Later there'd be the palliative excuses. Later the forgetting balm would be applied; the letter of the law would, as usual, be twisted and used by men of evil ethos. We were two men among many and it was by an accident of geography alone that we still had our sanity, we were still human beings.

I should have been cold; the night air was cold and the ground was covered in snow and I was not clad for warmth. I should have been cold; I was a high-ranking officer of the British Army and I'd trained my body and prepared my mind to be where I was, where ability could be my only weapon. I should have been cold; I had not eaten, from discipline, had mortified my flesh

110

to forge what courage I had. But I was blazing hot with an anger the like of which I had never known before, an anger that fed on the brightest fuel of all, the sight of man's inhumanity to man.

That night we found our way into the comparative shelter of those tin huts that had no glass, only gaping holes that did not impede the night winds that whistled down over the mountains and sliced like boning knives. The sergeant and I huddled close together, extracting what heat we could from each other and from the stinking cadavers about us. Miraculously, I slept. The sergeant slept too, and shortly after dawn I woke him. We got up from that mound of near-dead humanity and went to the door. There were other people walking about outside; I thought I recognised one of the newcomers from the truck last night, but I couldn't be sure, so alike were their fleshless faces. These were men who had tasted no food but skilly for two years or more, who had not been warm, nor bathed, nor even washed all that time, unless it was by accident. I walked all round the compound slowly, as if movement were painful, bending my body against the wind. The compound was like the minehead except that the U shape was sideways on to the road. I walked as far as the rocks and looked up at them, careful to see I was not observed. It would be possible to climb those rocks if one could store just a little energy, though I hoped we would not need to do so.

Along the side of the U and deep in the small valley into which the compound had been set was the lime-pit. From ground level I could see that the earth had been dug out of an enormous hole and piled on the other side of the wire fence so that a lorry could back up over it to tip its tailboard. Here the wire strands had been plaited together into one set. There was no danger of a break-out since one would need to wade through the lime to get to the wire. Elsewhere the wire was three concertinas

111

thick on three sets of iron stakes that looked as if they had been pile-driven into the rocky soil.

That's all there was. A circle on the ground containing nothing but tin huts and a number of human beings all trying to stay alive as long as possible.

That was the hardest thing for me to understand. Why did they bother even to stay alive?

The camp came slowly to life. The only sign of the passage of time was the movement of the cold sun in the sky, but shortly before the food truck arrived the prisoners had assembled in a ragged line that stretched back from a point near the gate where the snow had been crushed into flat ice. Each man was carrying a metal bowl. We had no bowls. I beckoned carefully to the sergeant and we started to explore. In the centre of one hut, almost directly beneath a hole in the corrugated roof, I found what appeared to be a bunch of rags. It was a man. He was dead, frozen rock hard. His bowl was still clutched in his hand and I had to snap his bony fingers to prise it away. The sergeant got his bowl from a dead woman in a hut further along the line. I went behind the hut, scooped the bowl full of snow and without being watched I wiped the rim, scrubbing it as clean as I could. Then I went and stood at the end of the line. By then the food dowser had arrived. There was no conversation in the line, and suddenly I realised that since I dropped into the truck on Voss shunt line I hadn't heard a single word except those the German guards had spoken in horror and disgust.

The food queue moved slowly forward as each man received his ladle of skilly. No-one waited for second helpings; no-one stayed in the lee of the dowser, which gave off a blast of heat from the oil burner below. Suddenly I knew where I had seen that dowser before: they were used to carry tar and asphalt for the roads. Back in Scotland they had been fired by coal, and the flames leaped from the back as the dowser was towed along. Asphalt and tar, in foot-round cakes covered in a white dust, would be dropped into them, and the workmen took the liquid off the back through a large tap. We would stand and warm our hands and watch the thick black sludge come out of them. And then we'd hasten home to the fireside and scones, smelling of the clean pine odour of tar and asphalt.

The skilly the German soldier put in my bowl was surprisingly tasty. Or was I so hungry my taste buds were starting to atrophy? It contained potatoes, and grain, and the husks of oats if not the oats themselves. And certainly there were pieces of what could only be meaty gristle. I had two in the bowl, each the size of a walnut. And there was grease on the surface of the liquid, and it coated my fingers when I picked out the solid bits, and I licked my fingers to get off the grease, and brought the steel cup to my lips to drain the last of the liquid and put my tongue inside to search for the last fragments of food when suddenly I heard a grunt beside me and felt myself pushed. I stumbled to the side and when I got the bowl away from my face I saw the lorry and dowser driving off, and the dowser, against whose warmth I had inadvertently been crouching, would certainly have swung into me and knocked me over if the sergeant hadn't grunted and pushed me backwards.

One of the Lithuanians spoke to me. I didn't understand him. I speak no Lithuanian. The sergeant did, and he replied. The prisoner looked at him curiously, or so it seemed to me. I was shocked and nervous because of what had nearly happened, and furious at the Germans because they couldn't be bothered to tell me to get out of the way. I had no value to them.

It is hard to comprehend that life can cease to have value, to accept that the tiny rules by which one preserves life can suddenly cease to exist. It's hard to conceive of a man driving a motor car down the centre of a crowded road without a glance for anyone who might be knocked down and destroyed on the way. I would have to take infinitely more care; I'd have to realise that so far as anyone but the sergeant was concerned I just did not exist. I was a machine into which fuel would be pumped at regular intervals. Tools would be placed in my hands and I would work. I would be taken to the place of my work and brought back from it. And that would be the sum total of my existence. If I grew ill, if I could not work, I would die, or be killed, and thrown into the lime-pit. Now I truly understood what the Brigadier had meant when he'd said I was expendable.

Dammit, I thought, I will not die. I knew I'd need great will, great skill, great cunning, if I was to survive.

The sergeant and I wandered over towards the lime-pit. No-one came to that part of the camp. We shuffled slowly along the front of the lime-pit and eventually under the face of the rock. There we sat down in a tiny hollow of snow which melted beneath our bodies and then froze again as if in disgust.

"What did the Lithuanian say?" I asked.

"He said, 'It seems you have a friend'."

"What did you say?"

"I told him that everyone needs a friend sometimes."

"Did he suspect anything?"

"Yes. He said you looked at him as if you didn't understand."

"And you told him I was touched in the head?"

"It seemed the only thing to say, sir."

"I wondered why you tapped your forehead ..."

"It's a bit of luck. He's been here quite a while. He saw us arrive yesterday and recognised you in the food queue."

"And wants me for a friend?"

"Apparently, sir."

114

I sat and thought. When they had eaten, quite a few of the prisoners had grown chatty, grunting in terse conversations I couldn't understand.

"Where the hell did you learn Lithuanian, Sergeant?"

"I was working in Kaunas before the war, the temporary capital. For Cable and Wireless. I was responsible for an office in Riga later, and learned Latvian; before that I was in Tallinn where I learned Estonian. But I still have a British accent."

"I've noticed that. Your Norwegian and your German are quite appalling."

"Yes, sir. I'm working on that."

I was cold and hungry, even hungrier now than when I'd been standing in line. I suppose all my gastric juices had been started and one bowl had not been sufficient to neutralise them. But that was no excuse for my bad temper.

"I'm damned sorry, Sergeant," I said. Dammit, I hadn't even thanked him for pushing me out of the way of that dowser. Did it take such a short time to turn a man into an animal? I'd only been in the camp one day and already I was behaving abominably.

"That's all right, sir," he said. It didn't help. He was too cheerful, too bloody imperturbable. The perfect Jeeves. But what kind of weakling was I to need such a man, such constant attention?

"For God's sake, stop mothering me, Sergeant," I said. I felt petty even as I said it. Why couldn't I be like the sergeant? We were in the same hole, weren't we? We'd both volunteered, and I'd known it wasn't going to be a bloody picnic, hadn't I? But he was always so bloody cheerful, even though he'd been brought up on eels and chips in the East End of London and looked as though you could pull him through the barrel of an eleven-pounder wearing his overcoat. Suddenly I realised the fourth reason the Brigadier had chosen me for this

115

assignment, the reason he hadn't listed but had probably been more important to him than all the others. He'd known damned well I'd take Bill Milner with me, and he'd look after me.

"Do you think you could find your friend again?" I asked.

"Yes, sir, he's in that second hut over there."

We got to our feet and shuffled round the camp to the second hut. I judged it to be about half past ten in the morning. Nearly dinner time, my stomach was saying already, but I tried to ignore it. We shouldered open the door of the hut and went inside. There must have been fifty people huddled all over the floor. There were no chairs, no beds or bunks, and the floor was inches deep in crusted mud and soil from the mine, almost like the floor of a deep litter chicken house. The temperature, however, was at least ten degrees higher than outside. One ring of bodies huddled against the outside walls where I judged the heat to be more, and the bodies spread out from them. Most people were lying with their heads on someone else's coat or leg. Another favourite position was flat on your back with your hands beneath your head and your arms spread wide like batwings or drawn up in the air beside your ears. One or two were lying on their sides with an arm tucked down the back of the neck of their overcoats. They were all within touching range of someone else. Two people in the corner were lying belly to belly with their arms around each other and their faces touching, as if they were Siamese twins, joined along their length. Our man was squatting against the end wall with his legs bent at the knees, and his feet tucked beneath a woman who was lying at right angles to him. His arms were folded across his chest with his hands beneath his armpits. Sergeant Milner squatted down beside him, squirming between him and the next man. He slid his body down

116

the wall of the hut until he was sitting on the ground. He hadn't been there more than two minutes before the Lithuanian started to talk, not moving his head, in the manner of prisoners everywhere. I sat on the floor Buddha fashion, my legs beneath me, my arms also crossed with hands tucked under my armpits. After a while the sergeant and the Lithuanian climbed to their feet and left the hut together. One or two people watched them go without interest. I waited five minutes and then followed.

They were sitting beneath the rock wall by the lime-pit.

"Your friend tells me you're not so touched as you seem, and you speak German," the Lithuanian said with a guttural, Nord-Deutscher accent, as I squatted down facing them.

"I have a pair of words," I said.

He smiled a thin, bitter, twisted smile.

"How long have you been here?" I asked.

He shook his head. "I don't know," he said.

"When did you come?"

He thought for a while. "I can't remember," he said, "I just can't remember."

"Where are you from?"

"It's a small place. You wouldn't know it. Priekule, on the Kurskiy Zaliv."

"So you remember your home ... ? In Priekule? You remember, on the Kurskiy Zaliv ... ?"

He shook his head again, slowly. "It's been a long time since I answered questions. I'm afraid I've forgotten how ..."

"But you remember your home in Priekule?"

"Only because, once, there was a man. He told me I came from Priekule. He was my friend for a time, but then he died, I think."

"The Germans brought you from Priekule?"

"Yes, so my friend said. The Russians put me in

117

prison when they came. The Germans brought me out of prison, and they let me work. That's what my friend said. We had a rebellion, which I led, and the Germans killed a lot of us and brought the rest of us away from Lithuania, and put us into a camp. That's what my friend said."

"In Germany?"

"I don't really remember. It was a camp. We did work. We worked filling gun cases. I was a yellow worker in those days, filling shell cases and my skin turned yellow. There were white workers, and they got bad chests like we did. And then I wasn't doing that any more. Now I'm digging in a mine, and I suppose you'd call me a black worker. Is this the same place, do you suppose? Are there yellow workers here, and white workers? I'm afraid I don't know too much about it, just as I don't know if it's true that once I led a rebellion."

"I bet you were a most important man," I said to encourage him. His eyes were shining. The hair had started to grow again down the swathe which had been cut from his forehead to the back of his head, and the gentian violet had been swabbed onto his forehead and had run down his cheek.

"I remember my friend; you know, I told you, the one who died; he used to talk to me about Lithuania, and we sometimes sang the songs of Lithuania. Sometimes he used to tell me about Priekule, and he knew my home there, but that might only be a dream I have, because we want to think of pleasant things, don't we, and perhaps it wasn't my home but only a home he invented for me because he was a very good friend and wanted to give me the pleasure of a wonderful home to think about. I do remember two men had a fight, and it was tragic, because one man remembered his home in every detail and he told us about it and it had an orchard and three bedrooms and he could remember it in every

118

detail and he used to tell us about it. But there was one man who became very upset, and he said he had been remembering his own home and it had no orchard and only two bedrooms, and he accused the other man of spoiling his dream by making his house seem inferior. And so they had a fight about it. I can't think why."

"But you can't actually remember your own home, only what your friend said about it?"

"No, I don't remember it at all."

"It must be a big and important house if your friend knew it."

"I haven't talked so much as long as I can remember," he said.

"That's all right," I said. "Talk all you want to."

"What's your name?" the sergeant asked.

The man shook his head and turned his wrist to reveal his number.

"Your name," the sergeant said softly, "not your number."

The sergeant would have coaxed him but I made him stop. Memory, once awakened, can be painful as well as pleasant.

"How many of the others do you know?" I asked.

"What others?"

"The other prisoners."

"The workers?"

"Yes, your fellow countrymen here."

"I know them all, except the ones who came in with you."

"Are they all Lithuanians?"

"Two of them are Latvians, from Riga."

"But you know them all?"

"Why wouldn't I? I talk to them all. They are all my friends, aren't they?"

"Yes, they are all your friends. If you ask them to do something, if you lead them, will they follow?"

"If I lead, they will follow, of course. If any man leads they will follow. When the food comes, whoever knows it is coming first, he leads and they follow in line. When the time comes for work, whoever knows it first, he leads, and they follow."

I tried to keep the despair out of my eyes. Are they so crushed they can live only as a corporate body? Have all traces of individual existence been starved out of them? The master race has its slave race at last, because wherever any leads, all will follow.

During what I judged to be the late afternoon, the repair and replacement of the generators was completed. We all heard the hiss of the steel wire cable running into the mine, the rattle of the chain and bucket system carrying the spoil over the fjord, the thump and rattle of the ball mill in the ore-processing plant.

A half an hour later the Germans came for us, ten men on the back of a lorry, all carrying Schmeissers. They didn't even bother to get off the lorry. The administrative officer came in a staff car with an electric loudspeaker system on the roof. His Feldwebel climbed from the car, took the microphone in his huge hand and started to chant. "Heraus, Heraus, alle Heraus." There was no need to say it in Lithuanian—we all knew what it meant.

Slowly the prisoners shuffled out of the huts and lined up five deep near the front gate. Each man carried his eating bowl in the pocket of his jacket. When we were all in line, the gates swung open, and we began to march. When we had passed through the gate, the Feldwebel yelled, "Halt," and we all stopped.

Two men got off the lorry, opened the back of the officer's staff car, and two Alsatian dogs sprang out, their handlers behind them. The dogs scurried into the camp and began running through the huts. It was a task to which they had become accustomed. They found the

120

first corpse whose bowl I had taken; then the second who'd yielded a bowl to the sergeant; then a third in the same hut. The man beside me was crying softly and I recognised him as one of the pair I had seen holding each other in their arms. I suddenly remembered that the other one of the pair had been a woman. When he felt my eyes upon him the man turned and faced the front. On instinct I touched his sleeve, but if he felt it he did not let on.

The soldiers dragged the corpses away from the dogs and flung them into the lime-pit. The dogs took one final wild dash all round the compound and then returned to the gate. The guard let them and their handlers and the two soldiers out. The Feldwebel put his stick across the ranks, dividing us into two sections. "The last section, after my stick, go back into the compound," he said. We heard them shuffle back and go inside. The barbed-wire gates were dragged shut, the German sergeant called, "Forward march," and we set off down the road to work.

I estimated that the march took about twenty minutes, so slowly did we go. The Germans guarding us with the Schmeissers made no attempt to hurry us. The gates of the minehead were opened when we arrived and we passed through them without a pause, along the railway track, into the mine entrance itself.

It was a chamber about fifteen feet high and four hundred feet long, lit on the sides by the electric bulbs concealed behind armoured glass, which seemed to absorb most of the light. We marched along the entrance gallery. At the far end the gallery divided into three tunnels, and without touching us except with a stick, the mine overseer, an Oberfuehrer, sorted us into three squads, one for each tunnel. He was the first person who addressed each of us directly, though he might have been speaking to a pack of hounds. "You here, you there, come along, look lively, you back there, you here, watch you don't

121

fall, come along, you here, you there."

I was in the same squad as the sergeant. Blast it. I had hoped we'd get a chance to see two of the working tunnels.

The ilmenite ore was in the rock face about a hundred yards inside the tunnel, which was eight feet wide but only about five feet high, so that one could not walk upright. When we came to the working face we found the veins of ilmenite had spread, rather like blood-carrying veins, in all directions. In this weak light, the veins stood out from the rest of the rock as a silvery section which, to my surprise, was crumbly to the touch. We dug it out with our fingers, as powder and small lumps, soft as flowers of sulphur.

One man was given a vein, which could vary in thickness from an inch to a foot, and he worked at the vein, scrabbling the powder behind him. Two men stood, or rather half crouched, behind him and cleared the powder away as he pushed it backwards, carrying it in their hands. Six or seven men worked to load the truck, and there were six or seven at the seams. Each seam had to be brushed carefully with your fingers to ensure no powder adhered to it. Our friend was working alongside me and helped in the whole process, explaining to those near enough to hear that I'd been brought up in Finland and didn't speak any Lithuanian. The Germans inspected the mine at the end of the shift, and if too much powder had been left clinging to the rock there was no supper that evening. He showed me the way to lick my finger to scoop out the last remaining grains where the seam thickened into rock. He showed me how to prise a lump loose with the ends of my fingers and gently place it behind me so the pickers-up could get at it more easily. And he showed me how to hold my face back when I worked a new pocket, to avoid the whiff of gas that invariably escaped when the new lodes were broken.

"Bad air," he called it in his Hochdeutsch.

Twenty minutes at the face and my heart was thumping in the 'bad air', my lungs were bursting, and my fingertips raw. I moved back from the face to make room for another man, and went back to shovelling the ore into the truck with my hands. I was in luck. No sooner had I started on the truck than the gear wheel at the far end of the passage must have been engaged, and the truck started to move away from me. "Go with it," my Lithuanian friend said, "to keep it steady. For fifty metres, you can sit safely on the back of it."

Nothing to do for fifty metres. What paradise. After fifty, possibly even sixty metres, I dropped from the back of the truck and crouched along after it to the end of the passage. The truck ran on until it released itself from the sprocket that was fastened to the steel wire cable. It ran a couple of metres further, bounced up against a bumper, and then, remembering what the Lithuanian had said, I pulled out the wooden peg that held the truck upright. The top was off balance when it was filled, and it tipped over, ilmenite, iron ore and lignite dust tumbling down into a larger truck below. While the truck was emptying I looked in one of the other passages. There they were not fortunate enough to have a tipper-truck railway, and the men were carrying wickerwork panniers of ore beneath their chests as they stooped in the low passage-way. I remembered the overpowering whiff of 'bad air' that ore could release, and was grateful I did not have to spend my day with my face so close to it. Now I could understand why so few men had come down our passage, and so many had gone into number one. This railway truck I pushed back to the mine face was doing the work of twelve men. And keeping us all that much further from the marsh methane, the slow killer gas.

When I returned, the sergeant was taking his turn at the mine face, scrabbling about among the thin pockets

123

of ore. I could see that he would soon not be able to reach far enough to extract any. Already he needed to press his face to the rock to get what few crumbs remained. In that position, he must be taking in lungsful of the marsh gas. Finally he stepped back, looking at our Lithuanian friend and wondering what to do. The Lithuanian examined the clefts, then went back down the shaft and returned with several of what looked like five-inch rods. It took two men to carry one. He placed the rod on the floor of the gallery, with the other side of it near the roof. Then he inserted a bar and started to turn it. As it turned, the screw thread ran inside the long bar and made it even longer, until the long bar was firmly fixed from floor to roof, and unable to move. Now the other men in the group brought some pit props which they used to line the tunnel from side to side, holding them at the top and bottom with soft planks of wood. One man returned with a truckload of screw jacks and two sections of the railway line. The line was extended over the planks we had laid as support for the sides, and then the men moved in with the screw jacks. These, however, were worked with hydraulic pressure. It was the same principle as the screw thread except that the inner tubes were activated by oil. Using these jacks the Lithuanians broke away the rocks which barred our progress one by one. It was a long, slow, arduous job, and not without danger since the rocks often snapped apart and flew viciously through the air. The rocks were stacked down the tunnel behind the shoring, acting as extra reinforcement. Oh to be able to swing a hammer, or use a drill, or chip away with a chisel. But the least spark, as we all knew well, and the whole place would go sky-high, and us with it. Even the hydraulic and the screw-thread jacks had facings made of alloy which would not spark on the few occasions they slipped and rubbed against the rock under pressure.

When the rock had filled all the interstices of the shoring, we filled the truck and I trundled it away. A German was waiting at the end of the tunnel with a dog, another German covering him with a Schmeisser. "Go back and let them all come out," he said. I could see he was scared as witless as I was at the sight of that gun, though I could see the German holding it had no intention of firing it.

I went back and told the Lithuanian to get everyone out. They left immediately. Obviously this was routine to them. When they were all out of the tunnel, the German sent the dog in, in case someone had remained hidden in there. After the dog had returned, looking, I thought, a bit green around the gills, he ventured inside. I could well imagine that no German would risk walking those passages with the possibility of a half-starved Lithuanian waiting for him round the next corner with a large rock in his hand. He seemed quite satisfied with the progress we had made. "You should try to get up into the top right-hand corner more," he said to no-one in particular. "Then you will have the room to get a good thrust to crack that rock on the bottom left." Then the two of them quickly withdrew towards the mine entrance.

Already I was tired. I had no way of estimating the time, but it seemed to me I had been scrabbling in that rock for a month or more. My back was aching intolerably from the continual stooping, from reaching out to pick at the rock, from lifting the heavy shoring props and the even heavier jacks in such a confined space.

"Every day, half the day clearing, half the day mining," the Lithuanian said, seeing me try to arch my aching back and wriggle my shoulders to relieve the fatigue. "Since it is your first day I will speak to the others," he said.

When we returned to the pit face he talked to the rest

of the team in low rapid Lithuanian, one of the oldest languages in the world, so the sergeant had told me. I could see that the sergeant was going to protest, but then the Lithuanian stopped him, and there were murmurs from everyone. Did they say no or yes? I couldn't tell. I was not shocked by my own attitude. I should have been, I suppose. Fair play, and up the team, and we'd eaten and bathed and shaved more recently than they had. But my back was breaking, and my fingers could take no more, and when they signalled for me to lie down at the side of the railway track and take it easy, I subsided gratefully, lying on my stomach my hands beneath my throat, my back arched as high as possible to relieve the ache. The sergeant was going to refuse at first, but I beckoned to him, and he gratefully dropped to the floor. Two other men from the last night's truck load lay down too. I watched them working on the mine face, then without shame I fell asleep.

It was warm in the mine, warm as a bed, warm as a woman's crotch, warm as mother love. I don't know how long I slept, but when I woke, they were picking out ilmenite again, and the truck was almost full.

The Lithuanian crouched down beside me. "Don't worry," he said. "We broke through to a very wide and very soft seam. They'll think we've all been working like ..." He stopped. He couldn't think of an image.

"What's your name?" I said quickly.

"Antanas Stankiewicz," he said without thinking.

"You see," I said, "you can remember. Once in your recent life you accepted responsibility to be a leader when you asked them to let us sleep; they followed you. Once again you were a human being, and a leader of men, as no doubt once you were in Lithuania, and so now you remember your name, Antanas Stankiewicz, leader of men."

"Who are you?" he asked, momentarily frightened.

126

"What do you want of me? Are you one of them? I've done nothing wrong except perhaps to permit you to rest a short while."

"You've done nothing wrong," I said, laying my hand on his hand. The touch seemed to reassure him. He turned his hand over and grasped my palm in his, looking searchingly into my face. "No, I'm not one of them," I said.

"Nor are you one of us!" Now that I could see his eyes from close up I realised that he was not an old man. His eyes were clear and fresh, the eyes of a young questing man still able to feel the pride and pains of his youth. I hadn't found him; he'd found me. By curious telepathy I had been found, probably by the one man in that fearsome camp still strong enough to help me.

"No, I'm not one of you, but I ask you to trust me, to believe me, and when the time comes, to follow me ..."

"To *follow* you?" I could see that idea was too large for him to grasp. It was too soon in the recovery of his self-existence to expect him to deal with such a conception.

I gripped his hand. "For the moment," I said, "just trust me, and believe me when I say I am your friend, and remember your name is Antanas Stankiewicz, and try to bring back only the good memories. And now we must go back to work."

I took my place at the mine face and scrabbled in that powdery ore that felt like Wensleydale cheese ready to break into crumbles if I handled it carelessly. What an archaeological fantasy to run this filler in between the granite rocks, like blood in veins, and then to let it cool and set like cheese, with only the constant slow movement of the rocks about it to rub it slowly over the ages and prevent it setting as hard as the rocks themselves.

The end of the shift came sooner than I had dared hope; no doubt my archaeological musing had sped the time away. We left when we were told to do so. As the last of us came into the mine entrance, the men and the dogs went back into the tunnels. The cold air punched into our lungs and we marched forwards with our heads down gasping for breath, coughing out our lungs. No wonder so many died on the way back to the camp after each shift; the change from warm air to cold was almost insupportable. I shivered as I stumbled along, avoiding the heels of the man in front of me, then, as we passed through the main gate and turned right onto the road by the fjord, I lifted my head.

It had taken the quisling only twelve hours to make a new contact at headquarters to replace Boghral. Twelve soldiers, alert in the back of the lorry, held twelve Schmeissers poised to shoot us all if necessary. The Gestapo officer was waiting with the quisling, and both of them were scanning the faces of the prisoners as we marched past. As I shuffled forward I looked into the quisling's eyes. Nowhere to run, nowhere to hide. She smiled her taut thin-lipped smile at me. Kari, the wife of Per.

Though I knew Kari had seen me, she seemed to be examining a man two places ahead of me with considerable care. She was standing six feet from us. We were now walking in single file, and extra lights had been hastily slung up so that our faces were clearly revealed as we passed the reviewing stand. Behind Kari stood the normal camp officers, the commandant, the administrative officer, the medical officer Klaus. Once I had identified him I was careful not to look at him again. As I drew nearer I saw a Gestapo soldier hold each prisoner with his rifle until a Gestapo officer permitted that prisoner to go forward. Now the rifle was pointing at the man two places before me, and Kari was looking at him, as if she got a sadistic delight from prolonging the proceedings. Sergeant Milner was behind me; she must have seen us both together. "Is that one of them?" the Gestapo officer asked, impatient.

Her eyes flicked along the line, from the man two before me, to the man in front of me, to me, to the sergeant, and then back again. She held out her hand, pointing with her finger at the man two before me.

"Let him turn and face me," she said, her voice firm.

The Gestapo soldier nudged the man two before me with his rifle. The prisoner faced her, saying nothing. She lifted her hand again, her finger pointing.

"Let the one behind him turn also," she said. The Gestapo soldier gave the man in front of me a slam with the butt of his rifle and he too turned.

Then her voice sounded, clear, and loud, and quite firm.

"They are the two men," she said. "This one in the front," pointing again with her finger, "is the officer. The one behind is the sergeant." The two prisoners looked at each other, side by side. I had not noticed them in the camp, and they had not worked on our shift at the mine face. They looked weary and confused, as we all did, and it seemed to me they had not understood why this woman pointed at them.

But why? Why was she denouncing the wrong men? I dared not look at her again; I could only bring myself to look as far as her outstretched hand, the hand with which she was pointing.

And then I knew why, and why she was standing there, and understood she was not the quisling as I had supposed and she was telling me so as plainly and as unmistakably as she could, with the Gestapo all around her.

When they tortured her, in order to make her agree to the denunciation, they had pulled out three of her fingernails. The hand with which she was pointing was trembling, and the ends of her fingers were covered in congealed, frozen blood.

*   *   *

I looked at the Gestapo officer, then at Klaus. He dared not catch my eye though I could tell he'd seen me. Somehow he had arranged to be at this identification parade, hoping to be able to do something, anything, on the spur of the moment. Kari had helped him by fainting. The rest of us remained there in a frozen tableau.

"Put them on the lorry," the Gestapo N.C.O. shouted.

Klaus straightened up. "With respect," he said, "I would suggest you let me look at them. They'll certainly need delousing before they soil the hands of any good German soldiers."

"It's good of you to go to that trouble," the Gestapo
130

officer said, no doubt recoiling at the prospect of bugs and lice on his immaculate person.

"And while I'm about it," Klaus said, pressing home his advantage, "I'd better take a look at this one. She'll be no further use to you if she dies."

I didn't hear the rest. The soldiers had come back to life and the nearest one clubbed me on the shoulder to drive me forward. "Heraus," he said, the only word he thought I could understand.

Antanas and the sergeant and I were squatting beneath the rock, not talking. Neither the sergeant nor I had anything to say. Each man thanks God in his own way in his own time in his own unspoken words. But I couldn't stop the image pressing across my brain like a nightmare, coloured, distorted, whirling kaleidoscopically in a pattern of bloody fingers.

The quisling had made his contact. "Two Britishers have come; I don't know why. During the past few days they have been walking about without proper protective clothing, sleeping out in the snow, and eating only a bowl of thin soup. They've dirtied their bodies and their hands and their faces, they've cut their hair with scissors, roughly, and trimmed their beards the same way." How long had it taken him or her to identify us with the Lithuanian prisoners? What had made is clear? When I'd pissed in my trousers and let them dry? When we were disposing of General Preise?

And since Major Boghral was dead, the new Gestapo contact had insisted on a personal identification. The quisling must have demurred at that—what happens if anything goes wrong, he must have said, and my identity is revealed...? It must have taken a lot of persuasion to keep him away from the scene of the denunciation. Only when he gave them Kari's name would they have agreed to his plan.

Kari would not denounce us so easily; they broke her spirit first by torturing her. The quisling undoubtedly thought that Kari was the weakest of the partisans; he had not foreseen, however, that at the final moment she would find the strength to pass us over and 'denounce' two innocent Lithuanians. It was easy to tell myself that the Lithuanians were doomed to death anyway—only this way they'd die more quickly. And would it be any worse than the long slow torture of the mine, with its inevitable marsh gas death? When they'd tortured the prisoners to find out why they—supposedly a pair of Britishers—had come to Norway, and had been able to prove beyond doubt that the prisoners were who they said they were, two Lithuanian forced workers, would they start to torture Kari again? Thank God for Klaus. He'd bought us time. And if the worst came to the worst, if my plans went haywire, he'd have bought the Lithuanians an earlier death.

The sergeant and I had nothing to talk about. I could read the anguish on his face, the double hatred of another accused on his behalf. I remembered how reluctant he had been to take his rest in the mine, knowing others must work in his stead. How many times had he taken others' burdens on his shoulders? How can you talk to a man like that, how can you tell him to let other, innocent people carry the load for a while?

"Antanas," I said, my voice quiet, "can you remember anything about Priekule? Can you remember? You led a revolution there, a rebellion against the Germans."

He started to tremble. "I've been thinking," he said.

"But have you remembered yet?"

I looked at the sergeant. He knew what I was after. He took Antanas' arm gently. "Antanas," he said, "you want us both for your friends, don't you? You don't want to be alone here again, with nobody to talk to, and nobody to work with, and nobody to eat your soup with, and no one to lie beside to keep you warm in the long midnight."

"Is that why you're here, to be my friends?"

Antanas' mind, I was convinced, was in no way impaired. He'd neglected his memory because of the pain it

133

gave him. If you compare today's portion with yesterday's, you cause pleasure or pain; mostly it would cause pain, and so his memory would blot itself out. Memory *is* selective. But when there's nothing good to select, memory buries itself, as his had done. Could I hope quickly to resurrect it? Damn it, I am no psychiatrist.

"Yes," the sergeant said, "we're here to be your friends. But you must do what we tell you, always, and you must help us, and you must not ask questions, and you must not tell anyone else what we say to you. Is that clear to you, Antanas, my friend?"

"Yes, that's quite clear," he said, and I could see he meant it. "You want me to trust you, do what you tell me, ask no questions, and keep my mouth shut."

I could have hugged him. If he hadn't smelled worse than we did! "I want you to stay close to us. All the time, day and night, here and at the mine."

We went and found a corner of one of the huts and huddled there together, getting what sleep we could. Because of the Gestapo inspection, we'd missed our food that morning, but strangely, I wasn't hungry, and snow had quenched my thirst.

That evening, when we assembled to go to work, the dogs found only one dead man. There was no sign of the Gestapo along the road, and the lights had been removed. Our seam proved to be deep as well as wide, and we looked forward to an easy night, though it didn't appear to make any difference to the others. The sergeant and I had been separated by the mine overseer, but by a stroke of good fortune, I kept Antanas with me.

When the morning brought the end of our shift of work, I let the others leave the tunnel, waited for a count of fifty, then took the wafer off my side where it had been stuck beneath a waterproof tape ever since I left England. I peeled the wafer apart as I had been instructed, turned the two inner sections together, pressed them and stuck them against

134

a rock above a lode of fresh ilmenite, from which the marsh gas was rising almost visibly. Then I hurried along the tunnel in time to join the last ranks of the prisoners leaving the mine. The sergeant and Antanas were also in the back rank, as we'd arranged, and we shuffled as fast as we could, keeping the back ranks tight to avoid stragglers. As we left the mine, the soldiers went in with the dogs. I looked towards the gate: with Teutonic efficiency, it had been swung open and four guards stood ready to close it again after us. We shuffled through the gate and went down the road, one German soldier on either side of us. I had noticed when I was on the hillside observing the mine that the night shift was always sparsely guarded in the morning; the Germans had camp duties, sick parades, cleaning tasks and breakfast to attend to.

Sixty seconds in a minute, and sixty minutes in an hour, but the wafer was timed to start to splutter in twenty minutes and that was a third of an hour and twelve hundred seconds. I'd already passed fifteen hundred and we were well round the bend in the road beside the fjord when the first rumble came. Be quick, be quick. Look at the sergeant. He's looking at me. The rumble started deep inside the mine, and then it grew and grew. I had been waiting for it and heard it first, but now it had grown so loud no one could escape it. I spun round on the ball of my foot, snatched the rifle from the German behind me, brought the butt up rapidly, one two three, each one a killer blow on his unguarded throat. He was still dropping to the ground when the whole hillside exploded. The mouth of the mine spouted a gout of indecent red flame, and black smoke poured outwards from a crevice opened by the force of the explosive, and then the rock slide started. It covered the minehead, blocked the road, tipped into the fjord itself, whipping the chain and the spoil buckets over the water like some daemon's crack.

135

"Tell them all to lie down on the road," I shouted to Antanas.

He obeyed by instinct, remembering everything we'd said to him in the compound that morning. Our German guards were dead, and we had their rifles. We dropped on the road, and aimed ahead at the bend; within a minute the four soldiers who had been guarding the compound came running. When they saw the prisoners lying on the road they probably thought they were dead; the sergeant and I let them come within our sights before we fired those borrowed rifles. Mine kicked high and right and I missed with the first shot, but before the Germans could get their rifles into firing position I had shot two of them and the sergeant had shot two of them. Three of them lay dead on the road, and the fourth stood there teetering. I put three more bullets into him before he went down, and two more into his head as he lay there, so savage was my hatred.

And now we had to move quickly.

The sergeant took up a position near the rock. They would never shift him from there, even when they worked up the courage to scale the smoking ruins of the mine.

I yelled again to Antanas. "Get everybody to the edge of the water outside the compound."

He obeyed instantly, barked orders, and moved them along the road like the sergeant-major of a pioneer regiment.

Mind calculating. They'll telephone to Voss. Headquarters will send emergency units who, with luck, won't arrive for ninety minutes. Since there is no road beyond the compound, they'll assume the prisoners are bottled in with four sentries and won't be in a hurry to get to them. I looked out over the fjord; four and a quarter miles long, and a quarter of a mile wide, the map said. Deep. Clean except at the south end of the prisoners' compound and the end of the gantry where the chain buckets used to tip. Now the gantry was leaning over the water and easy to see.

136

They were late. With the Hamilcars. I searched the ring of the horizon, across the tops of the mountains, south towards Norheimsund where the Germans had a battery, west towards Bergen where they had another battery, north to Voss, east to Ulvik and Fossli, two batteries too weak to worry us. The Hamilcars came from the south-east, over the mountain behind Mauranger, across the Hardangerfjord, keeping to the line of the Sorfjorden, then running south-east to north-west along the line of the fjord we were on. They came in high, very high, and since I had heard no engine sound, they must have been cast off some distance away, probably over the mountain, and already were too low for anti-aircraft fire. The Hamilcar was an ungainly beast, power-assisted, and designed to carry a thirty-ton tank. The Air Force and the Army had been experimenting and so far hadn't been able to make much sense of them, but they were the only vehicles we could use in our special circumstances.

They came in fast, then, over the end of the fjord, dropped their barn-door flaps. For a moment my heart was in my mouth but then I remembered these ungainly sods do that, drop swiftly, then level out. I could see the gleam of the pilot's cock-pit up above the snub nose. The Hamilcar dropped until it seemed it almost had to hit the fjord, but it levelled out and settled on to the water like an old lady into a deep chair. The floats held; they held! On Ellesmere we'd broken the floats off two of them, landing them on water this way, but the boffins had worked out a float strengthener, and here they were.

The skipper had started his engines during the last part of the descent, they fired, and he turned the nose of the Hamilcar towards the prisoners' compound. Suddenly I heard the crack of the sergeant's rifle. The Germans had seen the Hamilcar land and now the race was on. They'd be on the telephone to headquarters, headquarters would feed an 'urgent urgent' to command at Drammen, and within minutes the Luftwaffe would be on its way.

The Hamilcar arrived at the side of the fjord, and the front ramp dropped.

"Get the men into the plane, Antanas," I shouted. The sight of that large ungainly beast must have been totally incomprehensible to the Lithuanians, like a phoenix from Heaven. Let's hope it could rise again.

The Air Force sergeant who had travelled in the plane dropped down on to the float. What a job! Being towed in a glider all that way, for two minutes of fast and impeccable rehearsed action when you arrive. All the fixtures had been removed from inside the belly of the glider, and the prisoners surged forward.

The Air Force sergeant was untying the drums strapped to the floats, ignoring his passengers for the moment. We'd picked him to do this job largely because of his absolute imperturbability. He'd need it, when he was locked inside with that lot.

Each plane, we reckoned, would take a hundred men. They wouldn't have room to sit or lie down, but they were used to cattle trucks and tin-shed barracks and the inside of that plane would seem like paradise. The floor and inside walls of the plane had been lined with padded canvas; it would protect the prisoners from anything except ack ack fire and could be ripped out and burned when the plane arrived in England. I waved my arms to the skipper, a fellow Aberdonian with whom I'd spent three weeks practising this manoeuvre on Ellesmere, and he operated the lever that closed the ramp doors hydraulically. Then he opened the twin engines wide and the plane taxied until it was back in the centre of the fjord. The second Hamilcar came in, and the prisoners were loaded on to it. Then the plane backed away from the shore.

I heard the sound of the sergeant's rifle sporadically. He would have sufficient ammo to keep them at bay, and they could hardly rush him over that rock-pile.

138

Now the first glider had reached its position on the fjord and the sergeant on the floats dropped a drum into the water. The plane moved forward and then back at an angle, and he dropped another drum. A wire cable, supported near the surface on plastic floats, stretched from drum to drum. We had never been able to achieve a hundred per cent success with this part of the operation. The Hamilcar slowly backed away from the drums. I knew they'd be playing out cable from the winch which carried a hydraulic clutch coupling, and a hundred yards of extra tensile steel rope carrying floats and mounted in a specially reinforced housing on the nose of the glider. The second Hamilcar had meanwhile manoeuvred into position almost directly opposite the first. "Don't let the drums float into each other," I prayed.

The twin-engined Dakota came in low over the end of the fjord, a beautiful sight. I'd jumped out of Dakotas, dropped supplies to other men out of them. If a man ever conceived an affection for a breed of machine, I did for that aeroplane. It came in low over the south-east tip of the fjord, and already Hamish was winching his cable down. It was hanging from a hydraulic clutch at an angle of about forty degrees with horizontal. Beautiful. Just exactly the way we'd practised it. There was rifle fire from the camp beyond the road block, but they hadn't a hope in hell of hitting him side on. On the end of his dangling cable was a hook, a massive drop-forged steel prong that kept his wire down. The Dakota dived from the back over the Hamilcar, then, when it seemed inevitable that he hit the water, Hamish throttled back and levelled out, and the hook went straight into the water between the two drums, dead in the centre. No question that it would grab the cable stretched between the two drums; it couldn't miss.

Now we had a problem of hydraulics, statics, mechanics, all wrapped in one. The Dakota was travelling at its minimum no-stall speed, and had no energy to pull anything.

139

The Hamilcar, fully laden, was sitting in the water. If that hook caught a fixed wire, the Dakota would be yanked down into the fjord. A number of things had to happen in sequence. First Alexander in the Hamilcar had to give maximum boost to his assisting engines—big enough to move him forwards but not big enough to fly him—but he had to keep his propellers feathered so the Hamilcar didn't move forward and override the cable between the drums. Hamish in the Dakota had to drop his speed and dive at such an angle that the hook engaged in the wire. At that very second there could be no resistance on either winch, so that the steel wire would be free to scream off. One hundred yards of it on the Hamilcar's winch, another hundred yards on the Dakota winch, but at that moment the Dakota was travelling over two hundred feet per second, and the transfer of energy from the static weight of the Hamilcar to the mobile pull of the Dakota had to take only three seconds, preferably less. Alexander helped of course by feathering his props the instant the Dakota was over his head, so that when the hook took the line the Hamilcar was already raging forward. At the same time Alexander started to engage the clutch on his winch further to help the forward pull. As soon as the hook engaged in the wire, Hamish boosted the power of his engines to take the additional strain of the weight of the Hamilcar, and he started to engage his clutch to help drag the Hamilcar forward. And both of those clutches had to be fully engaged in a maximum time of three seconds from the moment of first contact. The Air Force said it couldn't be done, the Army said it couldn't. Even the Brigadier was against it, though we eventually persuaded him to get us both permission to try and the equipment to try it with. Hamish, Alexander, an engineer called Keith Semple, and I, on a lake called Ellesmere. How do men time an action together with that hundredth-of-a-second accuracy? Was it the drinking we did together in Keswick while we were waiting for them to replace the four wrecked Hamilcars and the two Dakotas we pulled down into the drink? Was it the three pilots we injured, or Keith Semple, whom we killed by letting him ride the front of a Hamilcar when one of those steel cables tore apart and the wicked ends curling back whipped the flesh off him?

Hamish and Alexander were tuned together more accurately than if they'd been Siamese twins joined at the mind. The hook caught the tow rope and pulled it forward off the float drums. Alexander gave the Hamilcar the gun, feathered his propellers, and the fat ugly glider lifted its belly in the fjord and started to lumber forward, the way they say an elephant does when it sees a mouse. I could hear those two auxiliary engines on the Hamilcar's wings, and their scream of protest as Alexander forced them up to unprecedented revs. Then the tow wire came up off the water with the twang of some monstrous violin string; both clutches were screeching and reeling off steel rope under the enormous drag of that damned great solid heavy lumbering glider loaded with bodies, and then the glider was running forward and skimming across the water, literally snatched into the air by the Dakota, and the ploughed waves dropped back, and the hideous screeches abated and gave way to the thunderous roar of sweet flight and the glider lifted clear and I could see light beneath its belly, and it was in the air lifting behind and above the Dakota in less than a couple of hundred screaming, heart-pounding yards.

We'd had all manner of faults on Ellesmere. Twice, for no reason Keith could work out, the nose of the Hamilcar had tipped and ploughed down into the water, crashing the Dakota. Twice, no three times, the wire had stripped the clutches, and once the wire had snapped. That was the time Keith had been killed. But this time everything held, wire and clutches and nose suspension and tail suspension, and the take-off was sweet and neat, the way Keith had always said it would be if everything could be co-ordinated perfectly, and the Hamilcar was balanced like a prima ballerina, floating across the sky in an aerial pas de deux that would have brought an audience to its feet.

Then the second Dakota dipped down. Alan Johnson, and Trevor Lennam, two good lads following two good lads, and they hooked, caught, yanked together, and the second Hamilcar joined the first, up in the air going due north-west, two Dakotas, two Hamilcars, and a couple of hundred Lithuanians for whom life, once again, could begin.

We were all alone, Sergeant Bill Milner and I, with six dead Germans, the crack of rifles behind the road block, and the insupportable overpowering stench from what remained of Lithuanian Forced Labour Prison Camp number N (for Norway) 577.

The sergeant and I ran down the road, firing an occasional round at the blockage to make the Germans think we were still there. A section of Messerschmitts came whanging down the fjord, looking for the Dakotas; I felt like standing up and shouting, "They went the other way." We'd been promised Spitfire support for the Dakotas over the North Sea and I wasn't worried they'd make it back to England. When we were a mile from the compound we started to climb, up towards a stand of pine in which I'd left our equipment and clothing.

Have you ever taken a bath by rolling in the snow? It was the most exhilarating experience I'd ever had. I filled my hands with snow and scrubbed my body all over. I had an ugly red rash between my legs, and what felt like crabs in my pubis. My body had been bitten many times by lice and bugs, and when I combed my hair, little squirming things dropped off the fine-toothed comb. We'd hidden a bottle of schnapps with our clothing and we used half of it to wash our hairy parts; it bit like acid, but we felt clean. There was nothing we could do about the ilmenite dust. It had ground into our pores even in such a short time, and only hot water, soap, and a lot of scrubbing would ever shift it. And my skin was in no condition to be scrubbed.

We buried our clothing in the snow and put on the clean stuff I'd hidden among the pines in a waterproof kitbag. White woollen trousers, white shirts, white anaraks, long belted parkas. Then silk gloves, then mittens, white woollen hats, and the parka hoods with white fur-trimmed collars. Two pairs of socks and skiboots. Then I just sat for a moment beneath the trees, letting the warmth of my body soak into the clothing. We strapped on our waist bags and skis, took the poles in our hands and climbed out of the pine woods. It was slower walking with the skis on, but I wanted no delay should we encounter a mobile death squad. We saw no one. By midday, we were ten miles away, heading in the general direction of Granvin, due east, and about three miles north of Loftheim, in the mountains.

We found a place where we wouldn't be spotted among the trees. The sergeant boiled some snow with his smoke-less fuel stove and made a cup of sweet tea with the tea, milk and sugar powder we'd found in our supplies in Ragnar's cellar. Then we ate a stew of a beef cube and compressed high-protein biscuit. I also sucked three barley sugars.

"You want to watch that, sir," the sergeant said. "If you'll forgive me for saying so, your stomach is empty, and you might make yourself ill if you put in too much protein before you've had some roughage and a natural bowel movement."

I reached across and rubbed his bristly hair. "Bill," I said, "when will you learn to stop calling me sir?"

"When I leave the Army, sir," he said grinning.

I would need to wind a bandage round my wrist before I could bear to strap on my watch and compass. I looked at the time. "With luck they'll have arrived," I said.

"England will seem a paradise to them, sir, after this. But they'll need careful treatment; it'll be a long slow business to get them back to health again. You wouldn't care to tell me why we went to all this trouble to rescue them, sir, would you?"

He had a right to know now; he'd bought that right down the mine and in that stinking camp. "You know how things are done in the Army, Bill. Nothing's ever neat and tidy. It's like a chess game, if you like. You say to yourself,

144

if I move my bishop, I can put my queen on that square, and then I'll be able to move my knight forward and attack the king. But the whole game starts by moving a small and perhaps insignificant pawn. That's how this operation started. The Norwegian government is in exile in England, but they keep a close watch on what's happening. Every week somebody escapes in a small fishing boat and risks the crossing to the Orkneys; it's not all that far away. And, of course, we have information coming out all the time by radio; and people crossing the border into Sweden to train with the underground police force that's getting ready to come back here as soon as the Germans show signs of cracking. The partisans in this area weren't doing too well; from all our sources we realised they must have picked up a quisling. Job number one, therefore, help the partisans get rid of the quisling. We discovered the quisling was working to one Gestapo officer. Job number two, which has to be done before job number one, knock off the Gestapo officer. You did that job, clean, neat, tidy, the way you always work. I'm not saying it was easy; we've been through too much together for me to say any clean, neat job was an easy one! Another thing—we need to woo the Norwegians. They were never happy about our failures in 1940. They were expecting large numbers of trained soldiers and we sent them a few territorials. Norway wanted to be neutral in this war, and in a sense we forced their hand by dropping mines in their 'neutral' waters. While they were busy protesting to us about our invasion of their neutrality, the Germans worked a flanker and wound up invading the country. So we've not only an obligation to do something, it has to be seen to be done. Here's another problem—you see how it all builds up as a chess game...?"

He nodded agreement.

"We've got to be careful that every job we do looks like an accident, or at least as if the locals had nothing
145

to do with it. It would have been easy to get the partisans to blanket that camp while we got the prisoners out, but that would have meant obvious partisan involvement and there would have been reprisals. The partisans were very effective in sabotage at first, after 1940, but the government had to issue a decree putting a stop to it because the reprisals were so savage. Bringing those planes down and taking the prisoners off in full view of the Germans will prove to the Germans that the job was thought out and executed by foreigners."

"But why did we tell the partisans what we were doing?"

"Back to job number one. The reason we killed Boghral was to force our quisling to make a new contact, but first we had to give him something to make a contact about. So we gave him the story about blowing up the mine. When we think about blowing up a mine, we ask ourselves about the forced labour gang, and since their lives are miserable anyway, somebody in England says, all right, regrettable, but we can't waste war effort saving the lives of Lithuanian prisoners. And he signs an authorisation chit, which amounts to a death warrant. Now, you might ask, why are we interested in this place at all? We're doing a study; somebody—and nobody ever knows who that somebody is in a case like this—decides that this piece of ground may have strategic importance, so we're sent in to clean up the question of the quisling. When we get here, we realise that the partisans need a token of our ability, an act of faith if you like, and so we knock off General Preise."

"You never did tell me where you got the information about the general or the information about the prisoners or ..."

"Believe me, Bill, I'm telling you all I can. *I* don't even know the whole story."

"But you know why the Lithuanians have gone to England?"

"When they decided to let the Lithuanians die, somebody at the War Office said, shouldn't we go into this just a little deeper? And they tried to find out who those Lithuanians might be. Then somebody on a policy board started to think. Lithuania was annexed by the Russians, and then taken over by the Germans, but what's going to happen to Lithuania after the war? Is it going back to the Russians? We're certainly not going to let the Germans have it, and we're not going to give it to the Poles, are we? Lithuania fought for its independence in 1918. Its first president—as you know from when you were there with Cable and Wireless ..."

"Was Antanas Smetona."

"Right. We'd like them to be independent again after the war. But for that to be possible, they need a government. And that's when a few more pieces are moved on our chess table. These poor bastards here—and it's hard to believe when you look at them now—were all civil servants in Lithuania. And a government needs civil servants. If we can get these lads back to the U.K. and they can be fed well and brought back to health, they could be the nucleus of the government of Lithuania we hope to set up after the war."

"So someone decides we'll get them out ..."

"That's right. We may as well try. We're going to be here anyway, rooting out a quisling; we're going to destroy the mine and ten to one the Germans will kill them all in reprisal, so we work out a plan to get them out."

"And that's when the Brigadier is brought in."

"And that's why we spent all that time messing about on Ellesmere."

The sergeant sat there, thinking. "It's a terrible thought, sir, that as human beings, as victims of the Germans and

147

all that, they weren't worth saving; but as civil servants and the basis for a government, as pawns, you might say, in a power and political game, it was worth going to all that trouble to save them."

"Would you like to be the one who decides, Bill? Would you like to pace up and down on a War Office carpet with a cup of tea in your hand, this term's bill from your boy's school in your pocket, a pound of sausages to collect for your wife on the way home if the butcher has any, and look down a long list and say yes or no to the question, 'Shall these men live or die'?"

"All I can hope is that they never realise they owe their lives to their ability to push a civil service pen!"

*   *   *

I prayed the ambulance would be where we had planned on the Granvin road which, at that point, was a twisting track with many opportunities for unobserved approach. Perhaps the Germans had already pulled the troops out of the mine camp. Perhaps Klaus had not been able to get away from the ever-vigilant Gestapo or had been posted away from the unit.

I set the sergeant in a stand of timber from which he would not be able to see the rendezvous with the ambulance.

"I feel I should come with you, sir," he said.

"No. This is one time I go on my own. And don't say 'take care' to me, or I'll brain you!"

I went forward alone. Way over on the left, lower down the slopes, I saw a German patrol, but I knew they wouldn't spot me dressed entirely in white. I took cover for five minutes while a woman driving a small fjord pony pulled a sledge of kindling up towards a remote stabbur.

I ran alongside the Granvin road on my skis, turned

a corner, and saw the ambulance, a green, grey and red slash among the white of the hills. The extra red cross was hanging on the back door, so I knew it was safe to approach. I side-stepped onto the snow-covered road and slid down it. Klaus saw me coming and climbed out of the cab and opened the back door. I kicked off the ski bindings and climbed into the ambulance.

"Congratulations," he said. "You made a good job of the mine."

"It ought to have been destroyed years ago."

"All that explosion, all that demolition, caused by one man in a few seconds."

"With a wafer the size of a half crown. You had no trouble getting out of camp?"

"I had a row with the Gestapo officer ..."

"That's not a safe thing to do."

"It's the one thing they respect. Bow down to the bastards and they'll kick your arse for the fun of it."

"Feeling cocky, eh?"

"Why not? The sight of that mine blowing, and then those two gliders dropping down like birds of liberation ... You've done a marvellous job here ... *ausgezeichnet wunderbar* ..."

I stopped him before we formed a mutual admiration society. No one man does a good job; it's the planning, the little men, like Sergeant Milner, and the two sergeants on the floats, and Antanas, who make good jobs possible. But also the bloody martyrs, like Kari and Ragnar.

"It was tough to get away," he said. "I can't stay long."

"How are they?"

"The Lithuanians or the girl?"

"All three."

"The Lithuanians are fine. So far. I had a soldier with diphtheria. I took a swab from his throat and infected them with it. The Gestapo have given me forty-eight

149

hours to get them fit for interrogation. The girl—well, she's been treated badly ..."

"I saw her finger ends."

"That's only part of it. She's been raped. Badly. Internal injuries. She's missed peritonitis by a miracle. I've told them she mustn't be moved, or she'll die of it. I told them I needed two weeks. They've given me one."

"Are they going to close the camp?"

"We don't know yet. The commandant spent the morning in Voss. Came back with his tail between his legs. They've moved a detachment of Gestapo in with us, and we're waiting for an engineer to come from Germany. A mine specialist. Meanwhile they've put the men on heavy duty. There's been a tunnel collapse."

"I know."

"Oh yes—one of your jobs was it?"

"No questions—go on about the camp."

"All passes and leave are cancelled. I only got out by saying I must go to Granvin for medical supplies to cure the diphtheria ..."

"Have you been in contact with U.K.?"

"Yes, but I had only had time to give them a One Five One."

They'd love that back in England. It meant keep a watch on my frequency on the hour every hour day and night. I can't talk to you now but I will as soon as I can. It was hell for the British operators, but far worse for the man in the field; it always meant trouble.

"Have you caught your quisling?" he asked.

"Not yet."

"If I could only get that girl on her own. But they guard her and the Lithuanians, and I guess they mean to keep the guards on until they take them away."

"Don't worry," I said. "I'll find him. He'll make one slip, just one slip."

"Anyway, you got the Lithuanians out."

150

"Yes, we did that."

"That really was marvellous, the way you blew up the mine!"

"It blew itself up. All I did was provide a spark!"

We laid our plans for the future and I got up to go. He seemed less drawn, less tense this time, even though he had the Gestapo sitting on his doorstep. He looked out through the peep hole in the back then opened the door. A blast of cold air flooded the ambulance and I shivered. Before I went, we shook hands. "May I say this; it's very—what's the word?—nice having you here," he said. "I don't feel quite so remote."

"You're becoming more British than Winston Churchill," I said as I climbed out.

Forty-eight hours for the two Lithuanians, who had diphtheria, an infectious killer disease. Seven days for Kari, and she, just missing peritonitis, would not be fit to move very far. It didn't give us long to work something out.

I still had the same nagging problem. Whom could I trust? Other than my sergeant, Kari herself, of course, and hopefully her husband, Per.

It was dark when we arrived at the wood outside Per's house at Loftheim. The door was open. This time my nose did not twitch. Instead of climbing the stairs to the attic we went through the door into the ground floor living room.

Per was sitting alone at the table. "So you've come back," he said. There was neither anger nor curiosity in his voice. The wood stove was burning in the centre of the far wall. We took off our parkas and anoraks, and I put two more logs on the fire.

"They've taken Kari," he said. "I came back the day before yesterday in the evening and found her gone. There were many footsteps in the snow at the front and back of the house, and the marks of wheels of cars at the front."

"She'll come back," I said.

"You don't understand. The Germans have got her. She must have been betrayed. They came in from the back; only the Germans would have the use of cars."

"She'll come back!"

He showed his first sign of anger. "You damned English," he said, raising his voice, "always so optimistic."

"I know where she is," I said.

"Where?"

"In the sick bay of the soldiers' camp at the mine."

"Have you seen her? Do you know how she is?"

"I haven't seen her; but I know she's all right."

"How do you know?"

"You must not ask me any questions."

He jumped up, came round the table, towering over me, ready to thump me with his knotted hand. "I want to know," he said, shouting.

I shook my head. "Per, you've got to trust me. We must leave this house, and you must trust me, and if you do, we'll get Kari back for you. Now sit down; we have very little time, and everything must be done properly. And you must help us, or we'll fail."

He sat down again, impatient, still angry, but containing himself. "No-one but you knows we're still here," I said. "The quisling thinks we are prisoners in that soldiers' camp."

"I thought you'd gone back to England with the airplanes. I've never seen a trick like that."

"You were watching?"

"Yes; we were by Hamlagrövann, on our way to Dale. Ola, Tor and I. We helped make the landslide that blocked one of the Vossebane tunnels."

"Until I give the word, no-one, absolutely no-one, must know we're still in Norway. Is that agreed?"

"If you say so. If it'll get Kari out."

"It will. Believe me. Now tell me, is there one single big raid you have planned?"

Per thought for a minute. "Not a big one," he said. "You know they're against raids at the moment, unless we can make them appear accidental, like the road you destroyed with us and the Vossebane tunnel."

"Who has charge of the radio?"

"I have. Look, are you certain we have a quisling? Wouldn't he have taken over the radio? Wouldn't he betray the house when we were all inside it, so they could catch us all?"

"That's where he's being clever. He doesn't want this group disbanded, caught, rounded up. Another one would take its place, and he might not be able to infiltrate that one. No, his policy is to 'neutralise' you. He lets you work normally, only sabotages your jobs when they might seriously hinder the Germans. I've no doubt the Vossebane tunnel isn't very important to them, and they'll clear the wreckage easily. But if you were onto something big ... Bring the radio and let's get out of here."

Sergeant Milner and Per carried the radio and the batteries between them and we climbed the back way out of Loftheim on snowshoes. I carried our skis. When we came to a col overlooking the village we set up the radio. When Per and the sergeant told me the aerial was pointing away from England, I told them to trust me and be patient. I set the Morse key on top of the set, wrote a message, and handed it to Per. "Send that," I said, "nice and slow."

"Shouldn't it be in code?" he asked.

"Trust me," I said.

He squatted in front of the set and started to tap the Morse key. It was obvious to me he wasn't an experienced wireless operator. I knew it would be equally obvious to anyone who might pick up the signals he was sending out, and I hoped that would explain the fact that he was sending a message in clear language without encoding it first. His transmission would not be heard in England because I had set the aerial in the wrong direction, but any German listening station in Norway would be able to pick it up. And since they were bound to have monitor operators who understood English, they would be able to read it. Anyone experienced in military radio procedure would also know that the message ignored the standard pattern for such transmissions, another factor that would convince them an amateur was tapping the key.

ABLE FOX ABLE TO BAKER BAKER BAKER I HAVE NOT UNDERSTOOD YOUR MOST IMPORTANT MESSAGE DUE TO

154

BAD RECEPTION STOP ARE YOU ON THE RIGHT FREQUENCY
STOP I WILL TRANSMIT FOR THIRTY SECONDS TO ALLOW
YOU TO PICK ME UP ABLE FOX ABLE

Then he pressed the key for thirty seconds, sending an unwavering note to which any listening station could tune its receiver accurately.

"You realise every interceptor station in Norway will now be listening to us, don't you?" he said.

"I hope so," I said, scribbling on the message pad. "Now send this, nice and slow."

ABLE FOX ABLE TO BAKER BAKER BAKER PLEASE REPEAT
YOUR MOST IMPORTANT MESSAGE OVER

"Now we sit here and wait," I said, writing again.

This was my problem. I wanted the Gestapo to pick up a message, but I had to make them think the message came from England. Their listening posts were tuned to England on directional aerials; they would know immediately that our transmitter was in Norway. Since there wasn't time to get our station in England to send a phoney message, and anyway I had no code in which to send them the instruction to do so, I had to convince the Gestapo I had *received* a message.

"Can't you just imagine them all, tuning their sets left and right trying to pick up what England is saying to us? Especially since you've told them it's a *most important* message," the sergeant said, chuckling. Per still hadn't understood what we were trying to do, but I was too busy timing the pause to tell him.

"Now send this," I said to him and handed him the first part of the message I'd written.

ABLE FOX ABLE TO BAKER BAKER BAKER RECEPTION BAD
STOP I WILL REPEAT YOUR MESSAGE TO MAKE CERTAIN
I HAVE GOT IT RIGHT STOP MESSAGE BEGINS

Then I handed him the second page.

Per saw what I written. "The Gestapo can read this,"

he said. "The quisling must have given them the code by now."

"I'm counting on that."

The message we had supposedly received from England and were repeating to them for accuracy read as follows:

011221 040537 342109 273042 100625

It was a simple one-off code based on a list of words or frequently used military phrases, each of which was numbered. I knew the list by heart; so had Ragnar Bull.

01—we are sending

12—a most important person

21—Norwegian

04—by parachute

05—to a dropping zone arranged by you

37—arrange the zone

34—notify us by map reference

21—Norwegian

09—this event will occur

27—twenty-seven hours from the end of this message

30—his duty will be

42—to co-ordinate

10—military activities.

Just to confuse the issue, I put the signing-off number, that is, 06, and followed it with 25, a figure that meant nothing and merely added to the confusion.

"Wait a few seconds and then send them a WILCO and OUT," I said. He did so. "Now let's get out of here before the nearest mobile death squad arrives!"

We hid in a deserted mountain hut high on the Graasiden. From it we could see the entire valley. Per left on his round of the partisans. He met them one by one, each time alone, and to each he gave a slip of paper bearing a map reference.

The map references were all different.

"Why not just send him round with the false map

references and the false message, sir?" the sergeant asked.

"Psychology. Obviously the partisans are suspicious. We've planted suspicion among them. The quisling will be suspicious until those two Lithuanians the Gestapo think are us have talked. He won't dare go near them for a reason I can't tell you, but he'll be on edge. When he is given that map reference, he'll get in touch with his Gestapo contact. By then the Gestapo contact will already have received a copy of the message we've just sent from his interceptor sources. The Gestapo will authenticate the message to the quisling, the quisling will verify the map reference for the Gestapo. And neither side will know they've been fooled. I hope."

"Now I understand why you always beat me at chess," he said.

From where we were sitting, half-way up the Graasiden, we could see each of Per's map references. Each of the seven was clearly defined and quite different.

How did the quisling communicate with his contact? By telephone from somewhere in Loftheim? That would be the easiest way, though of course there was always a danger of an operator listening in. But it would be difficult to do, because the post exchanges were all guarded by German soldiers, and the bigger ones were manned by the Wehrmacht themselves. Or did the quisling have a radio tuned to Gestapo headquarters in Voss? Hardly likely. It was equally unlikely that he would go into the headquarters in the village itself; it would be impossible to get in and out of there without being seen by somebody.

After the long midnight, the mobile death squads came silently into position in the valley and dug themselves in. One minute they were there, the next they were invisible. A second squad came in lower down the hill, and then a third. The map reference was ringed by soldiers, not one of whom could be seen. They were taking no chances. They had posted four men inside a hut at the centre of the map reference. They'd be the lucky ones, indoors during this long night, though they wouldn't dare light the stove. The sergeant had seen them all arrive and he knew the map reference and the name of the person to whom I had given it.

"Don't say anything yet," I said. "Let's make quite certain, first of all, that Per gave the map references correctly."

Part of the message that Per delivered was the same for everyone. "We'll meet at Vroligen's hut at 0400 hours. I will bring the 'important military person' with me."

As soon as the Germans were in position surrounding the map reference we left them to their long cold wakeful night and made our way to a rendezvous with Per in a wood overlooking Vroligen's. We watched the partisans arrive, one by one, then buttoned up our parka hoods and swooped down over the snow.

Ola was waiting outside with a rifle. He recognised Per, opened the door, and we all went inside. They were looking at us, Astrid, Anne, Tor, Bjornson, Aud and Knut. None had risen, but you don't expect Norwegians to have a slavish respect for authority. We unfastened the hoods of our parkas and let them fall on our necks. There were looks of pleasant surprise on every face. "You didn't go back to England," Aud said, and there was a gentle hubbub of conversation.

It ended when the sergeant and I took the Webleys from our coat pockets. We had them all covered.

Bjornson looked from me to the sergeant, from the sergeant to me. "What the devil is this?" he roared. "And where's this important military person?" Then it hit him. "I see," he said, "there was no important military person, only you two. It was another of your damned suspicious tricks." For a moment I thought he was going

158

to rush me. Per walked among them, collecting their rifles and stacking them out of reach.

"One of you is a quisling," I said. "I think it was Kari who told me I would have to prove it to you all in order to make you believe me, and now I can." My eyes moved over them. "Put your gun with the others, Per," I said, "because you're not entirely clear of suspicion." He did as I ordered, smiling. I had a shock waiting for him. "Today we arranged a false message about a parachute landing. Each one of you received a map reference for the dropping zone of a 'most important military person'. The quisling gave his map reference to the Gestapo. They informed the mobile death squads, who sent patrols to ambush the so-called dropping zone. The map references were all different. We can tell who gave the game away by watching the Germans." They were all silent, looking at me like schoolchildren waiting for the schoolmaster to explain the rest of the equation.

"By God, that's good," Bjornson said. "All different map references, by God. Of course, we never thought to check one another's map references. We weren't going there anyway; we were coming here. By God, Englander, that's clever."

"Whose map reference did the Gestapo go to?" Aud asked, her voice quiet, her manner tense. Slowly they all realised that one of them was actually going to be denounced as a quisling.

"We've just come from there," I said. "Any of you can verify this: go yourselves and see the Gestapo waiting."

I could see they believed me utterly.

"Which map reference did you give to Aud?" I asked Per. He took a piece of paper from his pocket and read out the number.

I turned to Sergeant Milner. "Where are the mobile death squads waiting at this very moment?" I asked. He took a large map out of his pocket and, not letting his aim falter, pointed his Webley at the spot. Then he read the number Per had previously announced, the one he said he had given to Aud. There was an instant hubbub, but no-one moved. Aud? It was, as yet, unbelievable! Then the sound of their voices died away, and Aud stood absolutely still, shaken, but outwardly composed.

"You are a demonic person," she said, looking at me. She turned to Per. "You see what he has done, Per, our Lieutenant-Colonel Gillespie. He has no wish to be directly involved in this matter. He knows that the quisling is our affair, and so he has arranged that one of us must denounce the other. You say you gave me that map reference number; but I know I have made no communication with the Gestapo, either this night or any other night. You say you gave me that number; and they say that only they and you and I knew what it was. I didn't tell the Gestapo, they didn't tell the Gestapo, yet the Gestapo are there. It must have been you, Per, who tipped off the Gestapo, since *I know, Per, that I did not.*"

Per was confused. He believed her, it was clear. The others backed away from them.

"If it's not Aud, it *must* be Per," Astrid said, looking at him with loathing.

"And it must be Per who gave Kari away," Anne said.

Ola took a step forward but the sergeant waved him back with his gun.

"But why?" Aud said, staring. "Why?"

Per swallowed hard. "You don't know what you are saying, all of you," he said. "You can't know. How could I give Kari away? I love her, she is my life. How could I ever give her away? I'd give my life for her. You all know that."

Ola looked around at the others. "Let's rush him," he said. "Let's kill the quisling, it's what he deserves."

The others pressed forward and I saw my opportunity.

Anyway, the farce had gone on long enough. I stepped behind them and rammed the barrel of my pistol into the real quisling's back. When he felt it, he stiffened. I reached into his pocket and took out the pistol he held in his hand.

"Yes," I said, "we'll let you do what you like with him. But your quisling is Knut Kierulf, not Per Vidgren."

They all turned round, and I pushed him forward. I thought he was going to make a try for one of the rifles near the door. For a moment I hoped he would do so, and give me the excuse to shoot him, but he didn't. He smiled that slow smile and when he spoke his voice was as soft as it had always been.

"How did you do it, Colonel?" he said. "I take off my hat to you, but how did you do it?"

"How did Per give you your map reference?" I asked him.

"On a piece of paper, with my name on it. I still have it."

"That's how he gave me mine," Aud said.

"You gave me a lot of strips of paper, one to give to each of them," Per said, thoroughly confused. "And then you gave me a list of all the numbers and all the names I'd given them to. This list."

"I'm afraid I deceived you, Per," I said. "You see, the list you have there *isn't* the true list. That map reference where the Germans are now waiting. You didn't give it to Aud; you gave it to Knut."

Bjornson turned on me. "Then why all this farce?" he said. "Why accuse Aud, and have her accuse Per? What a tricky bastard you are."

But they knew why I'd done it. The deception had caught Knut off guard. Once he saw me in that room, he knew everything was ended for him. When everyone was busy jumping Per, he would have found his gun

161

and escaped. I had to deceive them in order to get the drop on him.

"Why, Knut? Why?" Aud asked, pain in her voice. "My uncle was your friend. We were all your friends. We've known you all your life, here in Loftheim. Why turn quisling?"

I will say this for him, he was a brave man, and he had dignity even in defeat. He didn't whine; he didn't snivel or grovel. "I have never believed the Allies would win the war," he said quietly. "After the mess they made in 1940, I didn't think they could win. I made up my mind long ago that Germany *must* win. I still think they will win and I have been fighting for my convictions just as you have been fighting for yours."

"But my uncle, Knut, your lifelong friend. You were brought up together. He never harmed you."

"I know that, Aud. Do you think I don't know? Betraying your uncle—my lifelong friend—was the hardest thing I have ever had to do. For my convictions. We are fighting a dirty war, Aud, and the best we can do is to fight hard to get it over with as quickly as possible. Norway ought to have stayed neutral, even though the Allies were trying to force us in. If necessary we ought to have linked ourselves with Sweden. We should have accepted the Quisling government when the mandate of Haakon in exile was repealed; we should have been working *with* the Germans all this time, not against them. Instead we fight a stupid resistance that gets us nowhere. If only you knew the number of times I have persuaded the Gestapo not to take reprisals, the number of our lives I have saved. The Gestapo wanted to raze Loftheim after the first mine blockage; I started to work for them to prevent them. Listen to me, all of you. Our young men and women are being killed, fighting somebody else's war; our beloved country is dying. And what are we doing about it? We're blowing up tunnels, killing

162

Gestapo generals who are acting under orders from..."

I had seen Per pick up the rifle. So had Knut. Per fired three times and hit three times. Knut died on the floor in front of us, and we all realised that though we didn't agree with his thinking he had died a brave patriot.

It was a relief to return to being an infantryman, to work out a strategy for that classic infantry manoeuvre, fire and movement.

Our two best shots, Tor and Ola, hid among the cliffs above the soldiers' camp with their Lee Enfield rifles. Their longest range would be two hundred and fifty yards. The sergeant went along the road to the left of the camp, out of sight of the guard-house, taking Anne, Aud and Astrid with him. Per approached openly from the right, the direction of Voss, riding on a sled drawn by a fjord horse we'd borrowed. Bjornson and I skirted round the camp and went under the wire at the back. The wire was badly laid; it was obvious that they had never thought anyone would try to break in that way.

It was 0530 hours, when eyes are tired, and men on guard are sleepily awaiting relief in the half light before dawn. Earlier that evening the sergeant had climbed a telegraph wire to put the telephone and teleprinter out of action, and the radio hut was never manned during the night. Bjornson and I moved cautiously towards the back of the medical hut. Smoke curled from the stove of the cook-house and from a hut near the gatehouse. Two men on guard outside walked slowly up and down, not speaking to each other as they passed. In order to get to the front of the medical hut we had to pass within sight of the gate guard, but it was a risk we had to take.

Per came trundling along the road on the sled. As he approached the gatehouse the guards put up their hands to stop him, no doubt glad at the diversion, a break in the long pre-dawn boredom. They didn't even bother to unsling their rifles. All the camp was asleep except the cook, the guards, and the man at the console of the telephone exchange. Reveille, official reveille, was not due for another thirty minutes.

Now the sergeant would be moving closer to the gate. Tor and Ola, sights adjusted for the decline, would be holding rifles unwavering at their targets. Bjornson and I walked quickly round the side of the medical hut. Per would be giving the gate guards his act of being deaf, dumb, and dopey, all at once. We could hear them expostulating with him, still in good humour. This road is forbidden to civilians, they were saying. Can't you read the notices on the road? The road is blocked. Go back, go back from where you came.

But suddenly the guard commander, angry at being wakened from his uneasy sleep by the guard-house stove, came running out. Hastily the two guards unslung their rifles from their shoulders in an attempt to adopt a more military stance, and one of them started to move in towards Per. The two other guards rushed out of the guard-house carrying their rifles nearly at the ready, but by then we had reached the door of the medical hut, and Bjornson and I stepped inside.

The corridor stretched out before us. Klaus had described the layout completely. The first room on the right was the treatment ward. A medical sergeant slept there, preferring the comfort of the treatment bed to his plank bunk in his hut. He was a heavy drinker; he'd be out cold, not just asleep. The first room on the left is empty, Klaus had said, used only for minor ailments. The room in which they are holding Kari is straight ahead and then to the right; two Gestapo men sleep in the room with her. The two Lithuanians are round the corridor to the left, in the isolation ward. The German soldier died of diphtheria, and not even the Gestapo will go in that

165

room. Two guards sleep in the corridor, and it's not a popular duty. The rest of the Gestapo are just behind the guard room in the barrack hut they've taken over, and the detachment officer, a Lieutenant, sleeps in the hotel with the other officers.

We walked down that corridor in single file, Bjornson moving behind me like a large cat. At the end of the corridor I crouched, then looked left round the corner at knee height. It's an old trick. The Gestapo soldiers were asleep on canvas beds that almost filled the corridor, though they were placed as far as possible from the door of the isolation ward. Only twelve inches between beds and wall. Damn. Not much room to pass. Bjornson went the other way, towards Kari's ward. I looked carefully at the two soldiers in the corridor. Both were fully dressed, both had pistols on the floor beside their beds, where they could grab them the moment they woke. Part of the training of a Gestapo soldier is to fire a machine-gun burst over his head as he lies asleep, and watch where his hand goes.

Bjornson had placed his bear-like paw around the knob of the door that led into Kari's ward, and his ear was pressed to the panel, listening. His face was turned towards me. I eased my way forward in that twelve-inch space. The soldier was lying partly on his side and his head was back and up. When I was level with his waist, I glanced back at Bjornson and nodded. Now. Now, oh now I raised my pistol, still holding it by the butt in the firing grip, and slammed it down on the soldier's exposed throat. It's a killer blow, breaks the larynx and prevents noise. The second soldier came instantly awake, and his hand flashed down for that pistol in an instinctive movement. But before he could pick it up I had shot him through the throat. He was dead. The thunder of the Webley echoed along that corridor, and I immediately heard two quick shots from the ward Bjornson had

166

entered. I heard more shots from outside—Tor and Ola, Anne, Astrid, and Aud, and my own Sergeant Milner firing at any target foolish enough to offer itself. Their job was to prevent the soldiers from coming out of the huts, to give us covering fire so that we could move. Between the group on the hill and the group on the ground I was certain we could keep the German soldiers occupied. Fire and movement—one section fires while the other moves—the classic infantry manoeuvre they teach to second lieutenants.

With luck it could work. I opened the door of the Lithuanians' ward. The sweet smell almost choked me, and the knowledge that I was breathing an infected atmosphere tightened my lungs. The Lithuanians were wearing mouth and nose masks, as Klaus had said they would, but one of them had slipped. Klaus had offered me a muslin mask, but I had been afraid it would impede my vision. I couldn't speak to the Lithuanians in any language they could understand, so I shouted, "Heraus, Heraus." They leaped off their cots and came towards me. Klaus had taken away their blankets and they were fully dressed. I pointed to their boots and they put them on, then I led them back to where the two dead Germans were lying. I shouted "Halt," and they stood immobile while I tipped the first German off his bed. Bjornson came out carrying Kari, wrapped in all her bedding, and he placed her gently on the camp bed. I wrapped the German's blankets around her, brought the straps up from either side of the bed, and pulled them tight so that she couldn't move, wrapped in a cocoon. Bjornson smoothed the hair, that lovely long blonde hair, away from her eyes, and wrapped a blanket around her head, drawing a fold of it over her face to keep out the cold air, but not tight enough to suffocate her. She was unconscious, and her face showed the marks of her ordeal. I could see that she had bitten through her bottom

167

lip when they had tortured her.

The Lithuanians were in the way when we lifted the stretcher. I banged into them, cursing, but then I remembered their inability to think or move without orders was not their fault. We put the stretcher down, and I pushed past them and opened the front door.

Several bullets came whanging across the barracks and splintered the door. I slammed it shut again. "Take charge of these two comics," I said to Bjornson, "while I find out where they're shooting from." I pushed past the two Lithuanians again, cursing once more, and went into the unoccupied ward. The sniper was firing indiscriminately at the front of the medical hut, and two shots came in the window where I was standing, shattering the glass. I stepped back against the wall and waited for the next blast. He shattered the rest of the window but I had located him: he was in a hut just across the street. Because the hut had its side to the street, he was out of sight of the sergeant and the men on the rocks. I fired two shots at him, then snapped the window frame open and pulled it back. He fired two shots across the street, obviously saving ammunition. Stalemate. As long as he was there we couldn't get out of the medical hut.

I reloaded the Webley, then snapped two shots at him, and while he was ducking I took a flying rolling leap through the window space, tucked in my head, and landed on a shoulder sideways and forwards and sideways again. I came up at the corner of the medical hut. Now it was lighter outside and I could see what was happening. The sergeant had a good position commanding one side of the row of huts; Aud was on the other side, holding the soldiers inside by cross-fire. The sniper's hut was the only one they couldn't touch.

"Sergeant," I shouted, then placed my hand on head in the signal that means come to me. I saw a man in a window level his rifle as the sergeant dashed up the

168

side of the street, but two shots from my Webley and the German dived to the floor. I didn't kid myself I'd hit him at that range; a Webley's bloody useless at any distance. Ola and Tor had seen the sergeant run, and they pumped bullets into the huts as fast as they could work the bolts on the rifles. Aud was firing a Schmeisser; she ignored the sights and sprayed the sides of the building as if she were wielding a hose. I heard her change magazines twice while the sergeant was running. Then he was by my side, not even panting, and gave me a Schmeisser and four magazines.

"Cover me again, sir," he said, regimental to the core. I used that Schmeisser on the sniper's hut, and the sergeant ran doglegged across the street while bullets pinged about him. Then I stopped firing, for he was crouched beneath the window, pulling the strips off two grenades. He lobbed them in through the window, then ran down the street. I fired a burst through the window in case anyone was trying to play cricket with the grenades. I don't know what they were made of, or what they were loaded with, but the thump and blast lifted the roof of that building and blew out its walls and certainly killed anyone who might be inside. It sounded as if a bomb had dropped.

In the awed silence which followed. I heard the crackle of rifle fire along the road. Anne and Astrid were keeping the officers pinned in their hotel. They were firing only sporadically, so I guessed there were no heroes. Most of the huts were quiet now and the only rifle fire came from the cook-house. Men don't spring from sleep with very much bravery—the cook had probably been fortified by his early morning coffee and schnapps.

There was no way out of the medical hut except through that front door. I was cursing myself for not blowing a hole in the back of the building when I suddenly remembered the medical sergeant. He'd been

169

asleep in the treatment room but he couldn't have slept through all that shooting. With the sergeant firing rapidly at the cook-house to cover me, I raced along the front of the building and flung open the door. I heard a shot from the treatment room, and then another. One of the Lithuanians was slumped against the corridor wall, with blood on his chest and bloody foam on his lips. Bjornson stood in the doorway, his gun in his hand.

The Lithuanian was dead; so was the medical sergeant. I yelled through the window at the sergeant, and he shouted to Per.

Aud was moving up this side of the street. "Did you get the radio man?" I shouted.

"I got him," she shouted, "but I think I was too late; I think he'd sent a message."

Per had been holding the head of the frightened fjord horse. He had had to drag it up the street through the barracks. When he reached the medical hut, he let go of the horse and charged towards the hut screaming "Kari, Kari."

There was nothing else to do: I hit him on the side of the head with my knotted fist. "Get that horse, you bloody fool," I yelled. The horse was beginning to rear and tried to wheel in its sled harness to get away from the noise of the firing. They seemed to be shooting at it. "Get hold of that horse," I yelled again. "If you want to get Kari out of here ..."

I ran across to where the sergeant was crouched. "Got any more grenades?" I asked. He took two from his pouch and scuttled across the street, where he could give me better covering fire. Fire and movement, the instructions say, and now it was my turn to cross that street, to cross that open space that looked a thousand yards long, though it was sixty at most. I ran. I could hear the whack and wham of the bullets the sergeant was firing past me, and the tinnier sound of the shots Tor and Ola were

170

aiming from the rockside. If you run straight you keep speed but you give an unseen eye time to find you in its sights; if you run crooked you lose speed, as any rugby player knows, but you can't be bounced so easily. I ran straight and crooked, varying each five yards. I was looking at the open maw of the window before me; I saw the blast of a shot and they say that if you see the blast the bullet has already hit you, but so far I felt nothing. I kept running. I saw them crouched near the cooking stove under the fusillade from the sergeant, and then I was under that window in a long tackle slide and grateful they didn't have the sense to fire into the building from inside—the bullets would have come right at me, through that thin wall that separated me from them.

The grenades were home-made. A German stick grenade had been packed inside a piece of metal pipe and sealed with the plastic compound they use for repairing skis. The fuse was already sealed in and all I had to do was to strip off a piece of elastic bandage and pull a string. I had no way of knowing the length of the fuse, nor even if the timing would still be accurate, but I pulled the string and threw the grenade with all my might through the window in the corner away from where I knew the Germans to be. Then I ran down that street, crouching past the next building, my sergeant firing a steady rap rap of bullets into each window as I passed beneath it.

The cookhouse went up with a mighty bang. The oil from the cooker caught fire and spread wide, and the hut next to the cook-house caught fire, and I had started to run across the street towards the horse and the sled when I stopped a bullet in the fleshy part of my leg between my thigh and my knee. There's no pain at first. Just a thump on your leg as if you've banged it against the corner of a table. I could see the hole, and the blood started to well from it almost immediately. The pain came from the back of my leg and when I put my hand there I could feel a sticky mess of cloth and skin and thanked God the bullet had gone straight through. But had it taken a portion of muscle with it? There was only one way to find out. Stand up and start to run again, if you can. I knew I couldn't stay there sprawled in the street; other rifles in other hands would be pointing at me. I stood up. I couldn't run. The sergeant rushed to my side, but I pushed him away. "Don't bother about me," I said. "Don't bloody well nurse me. Go and get that stretcher out."

Per was in the hut, but the Lithuanian was outside talking to the horse, totally impervious to the bullets flying around. As I limped towards him Bjornson and Per came out of the hut carrying the stretcher.

Flames were coming from the hut next to the cookhouse and only our bullets, thudding regularly, were keeping the men inside the other huts. They would come running as soon as the flames started to spread. Four dead Germans lay on the threshold of the burning hut, a testimony to Aud's accurate aim.

"Move the sled, Per," I said. Believe it or not, he was standing there, holding his hand against her face where he'd removed the blanket. I rammed the barrel of the Schmeisser against his backside. "If you don't get that bloody thing moving immediately, I personally will pull the trigger of this gun and empty it right up your arsehole."

It didn't come out exactly that way in Riksmaal, but he understood, and he leaped for the head of the horse and between them he and the Lithuanian cantered it down the street and out through the gate.

Bjornson gave fire, and we moved; then the sergeant and Aud gave fire while Bjornson moved, and thus we all withdrew to the gate. Bjornson had been hit on the cheek; then the sergeant stopped one; it bowled him

172

over. I stumbled to his side but he lifted himself slowly off the ground. I fired practically over his head at a soldier who was poised six feet away. The blast of the Schmeisser took half his chest away and he went over backwards, gurgling and half screaming, and already dead.

And that was the end of the firing. We had licked them. The few who remained alive were cowering in those huts, tending their wounds, waiting for us to come and get them. I left them where they were.

We gathered together and took to the mountains towards Granvin, a painful bloody band of people. I'd been lucky. My wound would make me stiff as hell for a day or two, but I could still use my muscles a little. I strapped a field bandage around the hole in my leg while we walked along. I was more concerned about my sergeant. He'd been hit on the outside of his hip bone. The ball and socket joint seemed all right, but he couldn't move his left leg without pain, and we strapped him to the sled with Kari. The little fjord pony, sure footed on the snow, dragged them forward at a hell of a clip. Per walked beside the sled, looking at Kari's face. Bjornson tried to cover it several times, but each time Per drew the blanket back. Anne, Astrid, Tor and Ola kept watch for the rest of us, their Schmeissers still held at the ready. Bjornson, the man from Narvik, the hard man from the north, well, whenever the going got tough, he picked me up and, tall as I am, carried me like a baby.

We all knew the partisans would never operate again as a group. Too many people had seen them, too many soldiers would be able to identify them. It was also a certain bet that Knut had kept a record of their names, meeting places, code words.

We had come to the crest of a hill and were resting. Aud squatted beside me. "I didn't get the radio man in time," she said. "I'm sure he got a message out."

"It doesn't matter," I said, "and you mustn't blame yourself."

We were far enough from the camp by now to set up our own radio. This time it was on the correct compass bearing for a transmission to England. I tapped out a short message to the operator, then signed off rapidly.

We moved again, struggling ever upwards through the wooded slopes, across the snow runs, seeing the whole valley spread out behind us, ourselves a group of ants on its side. We went to ground when a spotter plane came over, and they didn't see us.

An hour later the Germans, with typical Teutonic speed and efficiency, were landing a stick of Fallschirmjaegers in the general area of the camp. I called England again, and the Brigadier himself was standing next to the laddie tapping the Morse key. I told him what we needed, and where, and when. He promised to organise it. I told him I'd keep in touch; he said yes, do that. I asked him if he had any news for me, and he told me the Strategic Committee had met and the results were as he had predicted. The area in which I was would not be used. I said bugger. He told me the Germans were getting you know what kind of ore from Sweden in large quantities, and I said bugger again. Then I told him that we'd got the quisling, just to make myself feel good, and that we'd all probably caught diphtheria, just to make him feel bad, and how were the Lithuanians? He told me the Hamilcars had both broken away from their tow ropes over the Norwegian coast, and both had gone down into the North Sea, and hadn't he said it would be a rotten job anyway.

And I said bugger, roger, and out.